DAY ONE

TACCARA MARTIN

Table of Contents

TABLE OF CONTENTS

Author's Note

Welcome to "Day One," the first love story to come out of the fiction podcast, Unmasked. Created and written by Taccara Martin, Unmasked follows the incredible journey of a woman named Kenya as she courageously, and messily, navigates the world of healing and therapy. In season one, you'll meet Obi Okafor. A man whose presence in Kenya's life initially brings center and calm, but erupts into chaos by the end of the first season.

Though listening to the podcast isn't required to enjoy this book, diving into the podcast episodes might provide a deeper connection to the characters and a sense of empathy for their journeys. If you're interested in immersing yourself in the intriguing world of Unmasked, perhaps even guessing who could be the subject of the next love story, head over to midcenturymodern.media to learn more.

Prepare to embark on a riveting journey with Obi and Isi, and their determination to find their way back to each other.

Dedication

For Alyssa, Kassidy, Lashawnda, and Ronya. May you never stop chasing what fuels you. May you never lose sight of the fact that you are the writer of your own story. And to Kenyon. Thank you for always covering me and pushing me to soar. You are my center, my Method Man to my Mary J...All I Need.

CHAPTER ONE

Obi

I'd always loved watching my wife do her thing in the kitchen. Stirring this pot here and flipping that pan there. Seeing her hands expertly handling each ingredient with such grace, while humming a familiar melody from home took me back to when we were kids in Nigeria. The mischievous girl next door, with the braided hair adorned with beads on the ends, was now a full grown woman. Her smile that could win over the coldest of hearts, and her chocolate skin that looked like it was dipped in honey, still had the ability to captivate me.

I was able to watch her preparing dinner from the living room since my condo had an open floor plan layout. There was no music playing, but I watched her as she danced to a rhythm that was all her own, and I still knew all of her moves. All her intricate steps, each twist of her hip, and every sway of her back–I knew each well. I had spent what felt like my entire life memorizing everything about her. Yet and still, even though she had been my wife for almost a decade,, there was so much more for us to learn about each other.

If you didn't grow up in Nigeria, our marriage would be considered unconventional, to say the least. Isi had been arranged to marry me by our parents when we were still just kids. Our families were from the same village, and her father, Chief Njoku and my father, Chief Okafor, fought in the Nigerian Civil War together. They had each other's backs and took care of each other while in battle. When they came home after the war, they returned as brothers. They married best friends, Temi and Tiwa, on the same day and had their first children only a month apart the following year. Those children were me and Isi.

Having grown up with our families being so close, we were best friends from diapers. Few childhood memories don't include her. We were so connected at the hip that our names became synonymous with each other. Everywhere we went, people referred to us as Obi and Isi. When our parents couldn't find one of us, it was because they weren't looking for both of us. So despite this unusual beginning to our marriage, everything felt so right with us together because, for as long as we could remember, we had always been together. Isi had always been family. She had always been my home. Even if she hadn't felt like home for a while.

"Do you need any help with dinner?" I asked her. Knowing she would probably say no.

My wife was old school in that she took pride in caring for her family. She treated cleaning and doing laundry as if they were part of her commitment as a wife, but cooking for her was a calling. And since hers were the only hands that were anointed for it, she wouldn't dare let anyone else in her kitchen. Nevertheless, every time she cooked, or did anything around the house for that matter, I asked her if I can help.

"Would you mind chopping this onion for me?" She asked.

I wouldn't have believed what she was asking me if I didn't see her lips moving. "I'm sorry?" I questioned. Because there was no way she was serious.

I stood up from the sofa so I could get a better look at her and that's when I realized that she was serious. I watched her pull out her favorite cutting knife, wash and dry it with a dish towel, then lay an onion and the knife on the cutting board.

I was getting ready to ask if she was sure when she paralyzed my thoughts by staring into my eyes and softly pleading, "Would you mind?"

She knew what she was doing. Ever since we were kids, she could always get me to do just about anything she wanted by asking me with her soft voice and looking at me through her big, copper brown eyes. Something about looking into her eyes made me not want to hurt her or disappoint her. And since I had done my fair share of both, I wasn't going to let her down by not cutting an onion.

Isi and I were married after we both finished university. It was decided that I would come to America to prepare a life for us and then send for Isi later. The distance was actually easy in the beginning. When I had gone away to London for boarding school, it was agonizing to not be near her. We'd write letters and beg our parents for Isi to be able to come to boarding school in London as well, but they always said we would be too distracted. They were right. But my living in America was different. We weathered this separation much better because we knew it was serving a bigger purpose for our future. I made it a priority to travel back home for holidays and special occasions so my wife and family wouldn't feel abandoned. Taking the advice of my father, I sent cards and lavish gifts so she always felt loved. For a while, this arrangement worked for us, just like it had worked for so many others we knew that had this same experience.

I had only planned to stay in America without Isi for four years. But those four became six, and six became eight. It was just different here. I was able to try new things, learn about different cultures, and experience freedom for the first time on a whole new level. I kept telling my parents that it was taking so long for me to reunite with Isi because we couldn't settle on a place to live, when in reality, we couldn't settle on how to live. I wanted to try something different from what our parents dictated, while Isi wanted to live within the confines of tradition. This was where we would begin to disappoint each other. This was how we literally and figuratively began to lose sight of each other.

"You cannot continue to allow your wife to go hungry, my son," my father would warn me. "If you allow a woman to be left hungry for the presence of her husband," he continued, "she is liable to starve and begin to crave trash."

I understood what he was saying. Just because Isi seemed okay with our then-living situation did not mean she was not suffering. I just didn't know how to satisfy her desires while honoring my own. So I used the time and distance between us to try to figure out what or who I wanted to be after being exposed to this new side of myself that had recently been awakened.

I used the kitchen island to cut up the onion with the utensils she set out for me. There was something so calming about chopping vegetables. The simple up and down movement forces you to block out all other distractions while you focus on cutting even slices. While I stood there chopping my stress away, memories of when Isi and I were last together in a kitchen came rushing back to me.

We were just kids, but I vividly remembered how it felt when Isi and I were learning how to chop onions correctly from her mother. She was preparing goat stew for a big Christmas celebration, and she asked if we would help her. After Isi nearly cut two fingers off, her mother realized we had no clue what we were doing and took the time to teach us how to do it properly.

Isi must have noticed something different about my expression because I caught her searching my face when she asked, "What are you thinking about?"

The question caught me off guard, but I couldn't help but grin to myself about the memories that still lingered in the back of my mind. I didn't answer her right away because I honestly wasn't ready to talk about the past at the moment. Reminiscing about fond memories had a way of igniting hope in someone's heart, and I wasn't sure that hope was what we needed right now. There was so much being left unsaid between us these days, and I knew it was unhealthy. But allowing hope to infect her, with everything else between us being on the brink of ruin, could devastate her far more than the silence between us would. Hope has a way of lying to someone, causing them to ignore the obvious chaos headed right towards them. I didn't want that for Isi.

"Just thinking about all of the ridiculous conversations I'm going to be forced to have at the ball this weekend," I lied.

We were attending the Mayor's Ball together the next, and I used my anxiety about that as a cop out so I wouldn't have to share my real thoughts. I should have known better than to do that to her, though. She knew me too well. She didn't call me out on it or give me a hard time. She just smiled softly and said, "I see."

She went back to stirring the stew that she had brewing, but I felt terrible for not telling her what was really on my mind. I don't know when I stopped being able to share my secrets with Isi. I don't know when she stopped being my best friend who I could trust with every piece of me. But somewhere along the way, where unadulterated trust once flowed freely between us, fear and caution had taken its place. Regardless of that, she didn't deserve to be locked out of my heart.

"Remember when your mom taught us both how to cut onions?" I offered.

The biggest grin appeared on her face as we took a quick mental trip back to our childhood. We laughed as we recalled the two of us standing side by side chopping onions, while Isi's mother taught us the history and significance of everything we'd prepared for a holiday feast. How our nonstop giggling quickly turned into uncontrollable crying because the juices from the onions got into our eyes. We laughed ourselves to tears thinking about that day, and it didn't take long before one memory led to the next. Before we knew it, twenty minutes had passed.

As my memories took me from the happy times we'd enjoyed as children in the village, through the events that lead us to the unfamiliar space between us today, my face drifted to a more somber expression. I dropped my head and was looking down at the knife when Isi took hold of my hand from across the kitchen island, intertwining our fingers. I stood there transfixed, staring at our hands for a few moments, trying to push through the heartache that followed every time I allowed myself to be close to her. Not physically close. We lived together so that was unavoidable. But I avoided allowing her to get intimately close because every time she did, our fights managed to get worse. My eyes traveled slowly from our hands to her face when I found her gaze fixated on me. There it was. The hope that I was afraid of encouraging. The hope that us spending a few blissful moments in the past could erase what felt like a lifetime of pain.

"I think we should maybe talk to someone about our marriage," she said softly. Tears began streaming down her face as she added, "There is still so much left between us, Obi, and I want us to try."

She did know what she was doing. She knew that by bringing me into the kitchen to cut onions, it would trigger an emotional response brought about by the memories of us when we were kids. It worked like a charm. Because there I was, faced with those big, beautiful brown eyes that I didn't want to disappoint. Beautiful eyes coated with warm tears that I was man enough to admit were caused by me. I didn't know how to respond just then. I didn't want to ruin the moment with my true thoughts about therapy. So I kissed her on her forehead and then went back to cutting the onions in silence.

CHAPTER TWO

Isi

I will never forget the first time Obi proposed to me. We had been best friends since we were children, and our families had lived in the same small village for generations. Every Christmas, our fathers would prepare Kola nuts for the celebration. Kola nuts were given to guests when they visited your home as a symbol of friendship, respect, and hospitality. Obi and I loved Kola nuts so much that we could eat them for breakfast, lunch, and dinner. That year, while our fathers were preparing for our guests, I had the brilliant idea to sneak some Kola nuts from the basket. Obi was scared, but he followed my lead anyway, even though I knew it went against his nature to do something so naughty.

Just as we reached into the basket of Kola nuts, Obi's father caught us red-handed! He lectured us about how important the nuts were for tradition and community bonding.

"By stealing the blessing meant for others, you forfeit your own blessing," Chief Okafor said in his thick Nigerian accent.

"Sorry, Chief," we both said in unison.

Then he ran us off with a stern warning to stay out of trouble. We just giggled as we ran away because we couldn't promise that we would stay out of trouble. Not the two of us together, at least. In the midst of our running, playing, and sharing secrets, Obi told me that he had slipped two kola nuts into his pocket without anyone noticing. Then he held one of the Kola nuts in his hand and looked at me with a shy smile on his face. He opened my hand and closed the Kola nut around it, then looked at me intensely and said, "Forever. Okay?"

I looked at him stunned and afraid to move because my 10-year-old brain could barely comprehend what he was saying, even though it felt right. The longer I took to respond, I saw the sting of rejection begin to wash over his face. Not wanting him to feel like I was rejecting him, I recovered quickly by planting a big kiss on his cheek. I held the Kola nut up, stared back into his eyes and whispered, "Forever," and then I ran away screaming, "You're it!"

Of course, we were just kids and no one really keeps childhood promises. But up until two years ago, Obi and I did. We promised that we would always be friends first and that we would always look out for each other. We swore that we would never let time or space be an excuse for not putting our love first. We made a commitment that family and tradition would be our guiding force. And despite all life's ups and downs, throughout our childhoods, a single word kept us on this path - forever. That's why I was here. That's what I'd been fighting for.

CHAPTER THREE

Isi

Tonight's dinner with Obi was like a trip down memory lane. An unexpected journey that rekindled the embers of our shared past. I knew inviting him to join me in the kitchen would take him by surprise, but I also knew it would serve as a gentle reminder of the bond we once shared. The laughter that filled the room, the stolen touches beneath the dinner table, and the intimate glances we shared over a simmering pot – it was more than I could have ever hoped for.

Every part of me wanted to rush into his arms, to remind him of the magic that used to exist between us. But I knew better. It had taken us years to reach this point, and I understood that recreating the enchantment of our past wouldn't happen overnight. Despite the current chasm of difference and distance between us, I could feel the old Obi slowly resurfacing, inching his way back to me.

Our nightly ritual before going to bed involved catching up on the day's news. Obi had always been one to stay abreast of global happenings, but these sessions also served as a crash course for me in local public affairs. With the annual Mayor's Ball on our social calendar, he'd been keen on ensuring I was well-versed with the who's who of Atlanta. After all, many of those faces were regulars on the news circuit for one reason or another.

"Do you remember who that is?" Obi quizzed.

"Of course. That's Alexei McClaren! You used to work with him, right?"

"Yeah. We were good friends back then," he reminisced. "Remember when we dared him to eat pepper soup because he didn't believe how spicy it was?"

I couldn't even respond because I instantly started laughing uncontrollably just thinking about it. It wasn't long before Obi bursted into laughter himself. Obi and Alexei were both first-year associates at their law firm when I first came to Atlanta to visit for Christmas. He and Alexei were both working crazy hours, so it meant Alexei's family would spend the holiday in Aspen

While the two of them had to stay in town and work. I decided to cook for the boys but as I served it I warned Alexei that the pepper soup might be too spicy for him. Alexei, being macho and too proud for his own good, dismissed my concern and took in three big spoonfuls of the soup. For about 3.5 seconds, he was fine. Shortly after, his face didn't just turn red, it looked like he was going to catch fire at any moment.

"He drank an entire gallon of milk!" I blurted out between laughs.

"To this day, I still tease him about that whenever I see him!"

He still teased him about it? That minor revelation jolted me back to the present day and sent my mind spiraling. I wondered, did Obi ever talk about me in relation to that day, or did he parse me out of the memories? Was there anyone else here in Atlanta who knew who I was, or did everyone still believe him to be a bachelor? Did anyone else know who we were to each other? As I was considering, he noticed my demeanor begin to change and perhaps he even knew what was coming next.

"Do you talk about me to Alexei?" I sheepishly asked. "Does he ever wonder what happened to the woman you once introduced to him as your wife?"

I knew it wasn't the best time. I was likely threatening to ruin one of the first good nights we'd had in a while. But I was desperately looking for a place where I mattered in his life. I was grateful that he had come to America to build a life for us, but I wasn't expecting to feel so invisible or disconnected from the life that he actually ended up building.

"Isi," he sighed. I could tell he was being methodical about his next words. "It's not like... I don't see Alexei McClaren all that often."

"So that's no," I snapped back.

The temperature shifted between us as if a fresh ice storm blew through the condo.

"I don't know what it is you want me to say, Isi."

"I'm not sure I want or need you to say anything." I muttered. "I'm just looking for an opportunity to matter to you again. That's all."

"Isi," he said, this time with more pain and regret in his voice. "I..."

I cut him off before he could finish that sentence. I could tell something was on the other side of that sentence that I wasn't prepared for, and I don't think he was either.

"It's fine, Obi." I said. "I'm going to go take a shower and then head to bed. Goodnight."

CHAPTER FOUR

Obi

"**Y**ou ready for the Mayor's Ball tonight?" My paralegal, Chance asked me. I had hired him straight out of law school last year, allowing him to get valuable experience while he studied for the bar.

Chance was an unconventional hire, or so the partners told me, because he was 35 when he graduated from law school. Yet, when he came in for the interview, he didn't try to impress us with test scores or grades like the others did. He came in with the knowledge of our then most high-profile cases and proceeded to list all of the ways that we could gain an upper hand over our opposing counsel. As if this wasn't enough to impress the partners, it didn't hurt that Chance was married to one of Georgia's State Senators because to lawyers, political friendships were worth their weight in gold. Chance was also Nigerian so, when everything hit the fan with mine and Isi's marriage, it was nice to have a mate who didn't judge me for the predicament that I found myself in.

I wasn't exactly proud of how things ended with Isi last night, and I hated that I had to leave the house in a rush on a Saturday. Chance noticed that there were documents missing from a motion that we needed to file first thing Monday, so we had to go into the office and get it straightened out. Before I left, I went to tell her where I was headed so she wouldn't be concerned, but she was still resting. So I sent her a text message, letting her know where I was going, and promised I would be back long before it was time for the ball.

"No I'm not ready, but I'm gonna go anyway," I replied.

"Is Isi excited to be getting all dressed up, at least? My wife can't stop talking about her dress, and I'm not sure how many times I can continue to fake my enthusiasm to be wearing a matching tux."

I chuckled at the idea of Chance and his wife Ayana strolling into the ball looking like a Nigerian Ike and Tina Turner. "I can't tell if Isi excited or not. She seemed to be having fun with the seamstress when they were doing the final fitting the other day, but the seamstress is also her cousin, so who knows."

Chance stopped stapling the papers in the file he was working on and, although I wasn't looking at him, I felt his eyes fixated on me.

"What, Chance." I said with noticeable irritation in my voice.

Chance took a deep breath as if he was choosing his words very carefully. "It just seems like you are more indifferent than normal about your wife these days. Are you even trying to work things out with her?"

"I mean, I guess we are. I am. She asked me to try couples therapy last night."

"Well, that's not the worst thing she could ask for. What did you say to the idea?" he probed.

"I haven't said anything about it. At least not yet."

Chance was glaring at me in a way I had never seen before when he said, "So let me get this straight. You've got a beautiful woman who, after everything you have put her through, wants to try and go to couples therapy…and your response was to say NOTHING? I'm starting to question if you even deserve her, bro!"

Chance was one of those brothers who believed that, since wives do more than 70% of the heavy-lifting in marriage, they should be treated like queens and be given whatever they want. It wasn't that I disagreed with him. I just always felt like my and Isi's situation was more nuanced than that. Yes, she's dealt with and tolerated a lot over the years, and I had no excuse to not give her the world. But our problems had nothing to do with how much I cherished my wife. I loved her with my whole being, and I would stop at nothing to give her everything her heart desired. I just didn't think it was unreasonable to have desires of my own.

After two years of living in Atlanta, I had gone back to be with my family for the holidays. Settling into the familiarity of home and finding comfort in the warmth of Isi's embrace was effortless. It was as if I had never left–and that was the problem. Being in America was awakening ideas and a type of drive in me that I had never experienced before, and I desperately wanted to share it with my best friend. My wife. However, her strong desire to have children and raise them solely in the ways of our culture made her consistently shoot me down by changing the subject to something that wouldn't cause an argument between us. She didn't believe in arguments.

Slowly but surely, I began to question whether or not Isi and I could fully exist together. How could this work if she only wanted to embrace Obi the little boy she grew up with instead of Obi the man I had become? From then on, I became more and more quiet around her. Sheltering in place within myself. Never fully expressing my desires or who I was. And since who I was who had hurt her so many times, I was trying to give her the world even while I was shutting out the version of me that allowed my crazy ambitions to come between us. I just wasn't ready to give her the therapy that she was asking for.

Chance and I finished up at the office, giving us just four hours to get home and get ourselves together for the Mayor's Ball. As we were walking out of the building and to the valet to get our cars, Chance asked me a simple yet piercing question. "If you're not going to give it your all, why are you there? Staying, especially in this condition, isn't doing her any favors."

I didn't argue with him. I didn't even say anything in response to the question. I simply shook his hand and said, "I appreciate you, C."

He knew not to say anything else. He just smiled at me and nodded his head as I stepped into my black Range Rover, tipped the valet, and drove home to get ready for the ball.

Obi

I have always dreaded fundraising events like the Mayor's Ball. The people, the politics, and the penguin-style tuxes that I was forced to wear made it all a bit unbearable. But as an entertainment lawyer in Atlanta, the fastest growing entertainment capital in the country, events like this were a necessary evil. An hour before the event was scheduled to start, I was ready to go, but Isi was running late. I wasn't too pressed about her tardiness since these kinds of events tended to bore me anyway. This was also the first time that many of my colleagues would be meeting Isi, so she was understandably nervous and taking a little longer than usual to get ready. Nevertheless, our car would be arriving soon, so I went into our bedroom to see how much longer it would be until she was ready.

When I stepped into our bedroom, my breath caught in my throat as I got a glimpse of her while she was getting dressed. She was standing there in front of the mirror after she had just finished applying some shea butter onto her golden brown skin. Her hair was swept up with just a hint of her natural curls cascading down her neck, and she wore burgundy lipstick that played up her thick, full lips. I watched as she slipped into a beautiful lace bodysuit that looked like lingerie–one that hugged every curve in all the right places. As I gazed, mesmerized by her beauty, she caught me watching her. Never taking her eyes off of me, she smirked as she rolled stockings up each leg before snapping garters into place with her delicate fingers.

I wanted nothing more than to take those few steps over to where she stood and wrap my arms around her waist from behind, kiss the back of her neck gently and whisper how much I loved her. The animal in me wanted to devour every piece of her because, no matter what issues or problems were happening between us, my body still responded whenever I had the opportunity to release all my inhibitions and just see her. But I owed her more than my animalistic instincts that craved her. She deserved to be made love to, and I couldn't do that properly at that moment.

As if telepathically hearing my erotic thoughts towards her, she turned around and smiled at me seductively. Time stood still, and so did I, as she walked towards me. In an effort to be respectful, I put my hands in my pockets and tried to train my gaze to remain eye level. But I couldn't deny my impulse to take all of her in as she seemed to glide in my direction. Heat between us built steadily, and I clenched my jaw in agony from trying not to react to her in that lace bodysuit. I promised myself that I would not make love to Isi again until we were in a better place because I never wanted to make her feel like I was taking advantage of her. But if she got any closer, if she so much as breathed heavily in my direction, I would lose every ounce of self control and willpower that I had left.

Watching her eyes take all of me in, stopping at my groin area for just long enough, I'm sure she saw just how little control I had left. She stopped right in front of me. Close enough where I could smell her shea butter-coated skin, but far enough to where I would have to stretch my arms to touch her.

"Do you like what you see, my love?" she whispered seductively.

I drew in a deep breath and bit my bottom lip, because words had escaped me. "Ye...Yes," I stammered in a desperate whisper because, just as all blood flow left my brain and traveled elsewhere, so did my swagger and self-confidence.

I knew I was in trouble when she took another step closer, planting her soft hands on my chest. "Your heart is racing. Are you nervous, Obi?" she flirtatiously asked. But it wasn't really a question. When she was like this–confident and seductive–she was irresistible. Impossibly irresistible.

It was apparent that I had lost the battle within myself when I grabbed her by the waist, pulled her in close to me, and tentatively, but passionately, kissed her. I was bound to ruin her lipstick, but I didn't care while I was teasing her mouth with my tongue and sucking gently on her bottom lip. She tasted like cinnamon and sin all at the same time.

"Yes. Yes!" she cried fiercely before linking her fingers behind the back of my neck and reclaiming my mouth.

We hadn't kissed or made love to each other in over a year. But this passion between us felt like we hadn't missed a day. Remembering my promise to myself, to not take advantage of her, I pulled away abruptly signaling that we needed to stop. I watched her eyes slowly peel open and she looked like she was being ripped away from a dream she wasn't ready to come back from. Panting, she hungrily begged, "Why not? You don't want me?"

"Isi," I sighed into her mouth, stealing kisses between my words. "Of course I–" before I could finish my thought or say anything else, we heard our driver honking outside for us and I let out an exhausted sigh. I knew we needed to get going but at that moment, everything else seemed insignificant compared to my desire for her. I needed her to know that.

I kissed her softly on the cheek. Then grabbed her hands and kissed both, one at a time, and said, "Later. We'll finish this later, okay?"

She smiled softly and nodded her head in the affirmative saying, "Sure, my love. Okay."

I watched her walk back into the bathroom and proceed to slip into her dress. A black, sequined mermaid gown with a tasteful yet enticing slit up her right thigh that looked like it was reaching for the heavens.

I didn't realize how hard I was staring until she demanded, "If you're going to stand there and gawk at me, at least help me with my zipper."

I snickered at the accusation and hung my head in mischievous shame before walking over to help her. I took a few seconds to take her in as my eyes journeyed from the small of her back, where her dress lay open, to the nape of her neck where I couldn't resist planting a gentle kiss. The zipper seemed to be sticking so, in an effort to not break it, I had to firmly hold the bottom of the dress in place, just below the end of her spine and above her rear. And as I zipped her dress up gently, I saw her back arch as if she was beckoning for me. Inviting me to take every liberty and have my way with her. I resisted the invitation at that moment, but I made a mental note to RSVP later. I drew in another deep breath because, goodness, she was fine. Then I exhaled in agony. By the racing of my heart and the growing discomfort in my pants, I could already tell that tonight was going to be a long night.

CHAPTER SIX

Isi

Ididn't think I still had any effect on my husband anymore. When we were first married, all I had to do was bite my bottom lip and gaze into his eyes expectantly for him to be all over me with reckless abandon. He used to be obnoxiously vocal about how he craved me and, once he started feasting on me, he wouldn't relent until he had his fill. So feeling his enthusiasm as he rushed to devour me, only to have him pull back with a haste that almost felt like regret, left me confused. We had our problems, sure. But this, the passionate love making that felt like scenes from a movie, was always our thing. And since we hadn't been intimate in more than a year, I couldn't help but wonder if someone else had the attention of the man that, at one time, could never get enough of me.

We arrived at the ball 30 minutes after the scheduled start time but not before dinner was served. We were seated at the table with Obi's assistant, Franchesca, his paralegal, Chance and his wife, and other partners of his firm. Everyone was extremely gracious, going on and on about all of Obi's accomplishments. And only one spouse was indelicate enough to mention that she had no idea Obi was married. Thankfully, Obi made a great save by telling everyone about our families and how we met, followed by the charming way he proposed to me when we were only 10 years old. He usually downplayed the arranged marriage aspect because he didn't want anyone to think he was coerced into marrying me.

"The marriage was arranged," he'd say, "but to love you is my choice."

I had never been around so many important people in one space. I kept anxiously fixing my jewelry and playing with my hair when Obi grabbed my hand under the table and then leaned over to whisper in my ear, "You look ravishing. Now stop fidgeting, okay?"

Yeah. He still had an effect on me, too. I blushed so heavily that I was sure my burgundy colored blush was now red. "I didn't think you noticed," I replied.

"Isi, look at me," he said while grabbing my chin, turning my head to face him. "I don't care what we are dealing with or what we are going through, I love you. And my goodness, woman, how could I not notice you?" he gushed.

"Wow. I–"

"Obi!" Before I could finish my thought, Obi's boss, Morgan Spears, came over to grab him. "Obi! Remember that new artist Ari Sphynx I was telling you about?" Morgan recalled.

"Of course. Is she here?" Obi inquired.

"Yes, and I hear she hasn't retained counsel yet! Go do what you do best."

Obi looked at me as if to ensure I was going to be okay without him. "Go ahead," I assured him. "I'll be fine by myself for a while. This is what you do best, right?"

Obi looked at me with a devilish grin, "That's not the only thing," he quipped. Then he kissed me on the forehead and went off to do what he does.

I couldn't help but be captivated by his presence from my corner of the ballroom. He looked so handsome in his tuxedo and I, like several other women in the building, could not take my eyes off him. Obi was the kind of beautiful that made you wonder if Beyoncé created the "Black is King" album after seeing him. He was six feet and two inches tall, with milk chocolate skin and a chiseled frame. The dazzling smile with perfectly aligned teeth was God just showing off.

I watched as he took confident strides into every conversation and introduction. Greeting and charming people so effortlessly. If this was the thing he did best that his boss was talking about, my husband had mastered it. I could feel my heart start racing when he glanced over at me and smiled warmly, almost like he was glad to have me nearby. I couldn't say for sure, but I felt like our brief but sensual encounter this evening broke some of the tension we'd been feeling.

Engrossed in a conversation with Chance's wife, Ayana, a familiar tune suddenly filled the room. In an instant, I was transported back to a traditional Nigerian wedding that Obi and I had attended together. The melodious sounds of Beyoncé's "Already" echoed in my ears, igniting a deep sense of nostalgia. I searched for Obi in the crowd, knowing how much we both adored this song. I longed to share a nostalgic moment with him, hoping to see that familiar smile as we reminisced about our friends' wedding. The memory of the dance routine we created for this very song, with everyone gathered around us and spraying us with money, made me want to do it all again. We were unstoppable on the dance floor, and I yearned to recreate that magic with him, to remind him of our journey together and the bond we share.

I was swaying to the beat when I smelled Obi's cologne behind me. I turned around to find him standing with his hand held out., "Can I persuade you to dance with an old friend...for old time's sake?" he said.

"Obi, No one else is dancing!" I panicked.

"Does that make you nervous, Isi?" He said while mocking the way I asked him the same question earlier in our bedroom.

I smacked my lips and rolled my eyes because Obi knew that I never backed down from a challenge.

"Lead the way," I replied. Then he grabbed my hand and led me to the dance floor where no one was dancing except for us.

His colleagues seemed shocked to see this animated side of Obi as they watched us dance and laugh at ourselves trying to outdo each other. Before we realized it, a crowd had gathered around us in a circle, cheering us on. Chance, refusing to be outdone, grabbed his wife and got in the circle to dance with us.

"I didn't realize you still had it in you!" I yelled over the music in Obi's ear.

He laughed, trying to recompose himself after becoming breathless on the dance floor, and said, "I didn't either! Come on, let's get some fresh air."

He took my hand and led me off the dance floor. I felt like the bell of the ball as everyone stopped and smiled at us as we exited. We were almost through the crowd when my smile was ripped from my face at the sight of...her. She was beautiful and petite and perfect in a strapless, champagne-colored, floor length gown, with a slit that reached the high heavens. I don't know why I didn't consider the notion that she would be here, but the pure shock, shame, and rage that I wore at that moment let it be known that her presence was a complete and unwelcome surprise to me.

Obi

"Kenya. I didn't expect to see you here," was the only thing I could think to say when my brain was telling me to run like hell to avoid this entire awkward encounter.

"I'm well, thank you for asking," she sarcastically replied. "My company actually does work for Alexei McClaren, and I thought I'd attend to support Georgia's next Governor."

"Glad to see you landed on your feet after being laid off," I replied. A few awkward moments passed when I suddenly remembered that I was here with Isi. I squeezed Isi's hand tightly and stuttered, "Umm. Uh.. You remember my wife, Isi?"

"I do. Pleasure to see you doing well, Isi."

"The pleasure is all mine," Isi responded purposefully. Some might even say her tone was petty. "My love," she continued. "I thought we were going outside to get some air. It's crowded here."

In that moment, I couldn't decipher what Isi was thinking, but her aura exuded nothing but self-assurance and elegance. As we reached the event venue's courtyard, Isi paused at a captivating fountain that graced the center of the area. Its mesmerizing blue color and unique design gave the illusion of a floating ball on the water. Lost in awe of the fountain's architecture, I almost overlooked the tears cascading down Isi's cheeks.

"Isi. Please don't. Please don't cry," I said sentimentally.

"You shamed me and humiliated me. Again," she whispered with her head hanging low.

"Is, I'm sorry. I had no idea she would–"

"You should have confirmed! You should have shielded me from this. From her!" she chastised.

She was right. Knowing who Kenya was to the city of Atlanta, I should have at least reached out to see if she would be there so that I could find a way to run interference between her and Isi. But it was too late, and I wasn't sure there was anything I could do or say just then. We began the night barely able to keep our hands off each other, and right then I was afraid to touch her or comfort her, worried that I might break her heart even more. So I sat there and watched her tears drip into the fountain. And If I had a penny to make a wish, I'd have just wished for her, for us, to be okay.

Obi

I met Kenya three years ago at a Beyoncé and Jay-Z concert. As an attorney on the team handling one of their larger investment deals, they'd invited me to the concert as their guest. Kenya was there representing one of her clients, Excelsior Air. I would be lying if I said she was easy to miss. There was something special about her. She had a sparkle in her eyes and an infectious laugh that made me want to know her.

When I initially approached her at the concert, I didn't know why or what I was even doing. She was busy talking to clients and different people as they came by her booth while I just stood off to the side watching her work. She had an energy that screamed freedom and joy, and I wanted to be near that. When the crowd cleared from around her, she caught me stalking around and asked if I needed any help. Well, I considered myself a good looking and confident man, but something about her seeming to see right through me had me stuttering and babbling like an idiot.

"I...I'm sorry but...you're kind of difficult to miss," I finally muttered.

We shared a few moments of pleasant conversation when she

told me she wasn't looking for a relationship right then. I took the opportunity to tell her that neither was I – even though that wasn't entirely true. I wasn't looking for a relationship. As a married man, how could I? But I think, after spending time with Isi and my family and feeling out of place with them, I was looking for connection from someone who got me. Someone who wouldn't laugh at my crazy ideas or dreams. And after spending 15 minutes with Kenya, she was doing just that. She got me. Effortlessly. Just by standing next to her, absorbing her smile and inhaling her energy, I knew that any type of friendship with her would be dangerous. So I found myself a bit relieved when she declined to exchange numbers or contact information.

A few months later, I was invited to the home of Chief Amajoyi, who was a pillar in the Nigerian community and a good friend of my family. He was turning 60 so naturally, a big party was in order. It had been a while since I had attended a traditional Nigerian party, and it was just the type of environment I needed to let loose and remind me of home. The music, the people, the dancing, the beautiful women adorned in aso ebi, their traditional Nigerian clothing and…her. Kenya. She was there, too.

My mind and my heart were simultaneously racing as I came face to face with the woman who captivated me the moment I laid eyes on her. I honestly had never thought I'd see her again, and I'd hoped I wouldn't see her again because of how easily I was drawn to her. I quickly turned and fixed my gaze elsewhere, believing that she wouldn't see me if I simply didn't look in her direction when…

"Aye! Ahunna. Just who I was looking for," the Chief exclaimed. "I want to introduce you to an old family friend. This is Obi. His father and I grew up together."

"Chief, I thought you only had one beautiful daughter," I joked.

"Lucky for you, I have another. Ahunna is my first born."

"Well, it is a pleasure to meet you, Ahunna." I watched as her thick, beautiful lips began to turn upwards to a grin but not quite making it to a full smile.

"Hmmm. I'm sure," Kenya said suspiciously.

"Ahunna, be nice to him. He's one of the good ones. I'll leave you two to get to know one another," the Chief exclaimed.

As he snuck off, ducking and running like he had just dropped a grenade and was rushing to get away from the blast, I laughed at Kenya's obvious annoyance at this entire situation.

"So we meet again," I said, obviously flirting, and we both fell out laughing.

We became friends pretty quickly after that. It started by sharing witty text messages back and forth and funny memes throughout our crazy busy days. Then we began talking on the phone every night before bed. She became a part of my daily routines and habits that were unique to my growing desires and evolving views since moving to Atlanta. I noticed a bond begin to blossom between us once we realized that we had more in common than either of us imagined. We both came from strong Ibo families in Nigeria, both had fathers with unbearably high expectations, oth had dreams and ideas that our traditional families rejected or made us feel were impossible. Over time, after about six months of hiding and ignoring our attraction, our friendship became something more. Despite the fact that she had explicitly told me she wasn't looking for a relationship, and I wasn't at all available for one, we found ourselves falling desperately, dangerously in love with each other.

Months turned into a year after Kenya suddenly became a fixture in my life. We were friends that understood each other. Partners that supported each other. Lovers that motivated each other to reach for more. And even though there was an undeniable passion for each other, we never had sex. Well, except for that one time, but I'll revisit that later. If I'm being honest, I tricked myself into believing that the absence of sex justified the relationship. I allowed that idea to relieve most of the guilt I felt for allowing myself to get this close to her.

Kenya had been through a great deal of pain and heartbreak in relationships, so she said she became celibate to reconnect with her faith and her relationship with God. However, it was pretty apparent to me that the decision to be celibate had more to do with shielding her heart from more hurt than her faith-based beliefs. It wasn't the type of celibate relationship where sex was never discussed or kissing was off limits. We kissed and played and took things just far enough to know that we desired each other, painfully. But she was committed to her decision, and that allowed me to remain mostly committed to Isi.

While I was seeing Kenya, I still made the trip home during holiday times. However, my usual calls back home and the generous gifts I would send my wife started to dwindle. There was a part of me that really wanted to let Kenya in on my life back in Nigeria, on my marriage to Isi, but something – or rather, everything – kept me from doing so.

It wasn't just the fear of possibly losing Kenya that held me back. It was the fear of being judged for keeping this massive secret from the outset and for being unfaithful to Isi all this time. The weight of not telling her ate at me every single day, but I knew there was no escaping this situation without causing someone a lot of pain.

So the days slowly turned into weeks, and those weeks eventually became months. Before I knew it, almost two entire years had flown by.

I wasn't this guy. I wasn't dishonest, I had never cheated on any woman in my life, and I certainly hadn't been the kind of man who would bring a woman down this road with me knowing that the only end would be pain and destruction. I was the kid who adults always came to for answers because they knew I wouldn't lie. I was the teenager who fought my friends when they disrespected women in my presence. I was the man who did everything my father told me to do because I believed so fiercely in living out the honor and respect that I was taught to carry for my parents. So I walked through every day in agony, wondering which would come first–would Kenya accidentally find out about Isi or would they somehow, coincidentally, come to find out about each other? Turns out, it was the latter.

Isi

Growing up in Nigeria, you'd often hear tales from women who found out their husbands had been leading double lives in America, while they patiently waited for them back home. Months, sometimes years would pass before the truth would come out – the men had other relationships, even other wives and children with different women. It used to make my blood boil, how these indiscretions were often brushed under the rug, just because the men sent money home and took care of their families.

Obi promised me we would never end up like that, and I believed him. Not just because he said so, but because it didn't seem like something Obi would ever do. He was a good man. Always thinking of others before himself. Always considerate. Always kind.

He didn't know it, but I had found out about Kenya three months before the day that she confronted Obi about me. I was rejoining social media after taking a yearlong break from all the drama and competitiveness that it tended to breed. Obi had an aversion to social media because he was such a private person. So it was no surprise that he did not have a social media presence, outside of LinkedIn. That didn't keep me from following his friends, especially those in the United States. Yes, I would sometimes peruse the pages of his friends to see what he was up to. But I also wanted to know what the world was like that he seemed to have assimilated into so well.

One day while scrolling Instagram, I stumbled upon a photo of Obi's friend, Alexei, posing with a striking woman. The woman wore a blue strapless cocktail dress that complimented her sparkling blue eyes and dark hair. It was a beautiful picture, so I double-tapped the screen to "like" it. I was about to keep scrolling when I happened to catch a glimpse of the people in the background of Alexei's picture. There was a man who looked a lot like Obi kissing a woman on the mouth. Even though it was a still image, it was easy to see that the kiss was passionate and intimate in a way that I had only known Obi to kiss me.

I was certain that my eyes were playing tricks on me, but when I read the caption on Alexei's photo, it confirmed my suspicions. The caption read, "Got the pleasure of escorting this beautiful woman as my date tonight. Pic would have been perfect if Obi and Kenya weren't photo bombing us with their PDA!"

I must have read that caption a thousand times as I sat breathless and motionless. Of all the emotions and feelings flowing through me at that moment, anger, betrayal, humiliation, despair, confusion, the most jarring was disbelief. I honestly could not believe that the man I had pledged my heart to at 10 years old had abandoned me for her. Suddenly, everything began to make sense. The missed calls, extended periods of silence between visits, the lack of text messages and gifts he used to send. He was being occupied by the presence and comfort of another while I was left alone. With no one.

I went to speak with both Obi's mother and my own to let them know I was preparing to divorce him. The betrayal was too great. The hurt was too strong.

"If I don't divorce him, I will murder him!" I screamed through my tears. I sobbed in my mother's arms while Obi's mom made me tea.

"My child," my mother comforted. "You are understandably furious. And you have every right to abandon your marriage the way he has abandoned you. But I beg you to reconsider. These are the sacrifices we sometimes make for the sake of our family. For legacy."

Obi's mother silently agreed and delicately placed a cup of tea in my hands before joining us at the kitchen table saying, "We send our men out into a foreign world and expect them to return to us spotless. When the reality is, we just need them to return home."

"So, what?" I barked. "Are you saying that I'm just supposed to be okay with my husband galivanting with some strange woman while publicly humiliating me?"

"We are saying that Obi loves you," my mother chimed in. "And if your husband has not initiated these proceedings, then this means that, while he has made misjudgments along the way, his intentions are to return home to you."

I couldn't believe what I was hearing. I stared at them both blankly as I searched their eyes for a sign that they were joking. But neither so much as blinked in the direction of laughter, so it meant that they were actually serious. Two of the strongest women I knew–women who ruled their homes with an iron fist and took no mess from anyone–were asking me to roll over and accept my husband cheating on me?! This was not the stone ages. This was not during a time where women had no choices. I was a college educated woman with goals and aspirations of my own. I had plans to begin a jewelry line and had all but secured everything I needed to begin making and selling my own designs when I was asked to return home while Obi went to America. Why was I expected to forego my dreams while he got to go out into the world and play as if he had no wife or obligations?

The mothers were understanding but held firm in their opinions. They drew me a milk and honey bath and bathed me while I sobbed. They prayed for my sanity and peace while I lay sleeping on my mother's couch. They even sat with me while I stalked every social media page Kenya had and made smug comments about her. I'm not proud of that, but it was therapeutic. And after two weeks of stalking Kenya and sulking on my mother's couch, I came to a new conclusion about my marriage. When the time came and my husband returned to me, I would not leave him. I would not embarrass him. But I would not make the consequences of his choices easy on him.

CHAPTER EIGHT

Obi

After we returned home from the ball, we went nearly an entire week without really speaking to each other. I tried going to her once we got home that night, but she said she couldn't bear to look at me after what happened. It was as if the betrayal had happened all over again and she needed space. So I sat on the edge of the bed in our bedroom and watched her as she stuffed some clothes and toiletries into a duffle bag while tears flowed down her beautiful, brown face. She was going to move into the guest bedroom, even though I had offered to give her the master bedroom while I moved into the guestroom. But she refused.

She zipped her brown furry bag and began walking out of the bedroom door when she turned to me with tears in her eyes and said, "I don't know how many more times I can deal with you breaking my heart."

Four days went by, and we didn't say more than a few words to each other. She continued to make dinner and was always on top of things around the house, but she made herself scarce, disappearing into her bedroom as soon as I came home from work. I just wish she knew that I didn't care how dirty the house was if I couldn't talk to her and air all of this out. But Nigerian tradition had her believing that the archaic mentality of a wife cooking, cleaning, and serving her husband would be what held our marriage together. I didn't know how to persuade her against those beliefs without being offensive to our culture. I just knew that I didn't want a servant. I wanted my best friend back. And I wanted… no…needed to be able to fight and scream and cry to get back to who we were.

Isi always remained pleasant and pliable because she didn't believe in arguing. She never saw her parents argue or fight and, since she idolized their relationship, that meant she would never allow things between us to verbally escalate either. What she did see in her home was silence. I recognized the sentiment from my own mother. Women would go silent for days or even weeks, seeing how long they could punish their spouse for whatever they felt he had done wrong. I used to hear my mom bragging about her stamina of silence as if it was an olympic sport. Women would then pass this "sport" down to their daughters for them to master.

It was no wonder that Isi, in her full Nigerian strength, used her silence as a weapon against me. It definitely worked because her silence hurt me more than harmful words ever could. There were times where I would have rather just had the fight and said whatever we were feeling because at least we would know where the other stood mentally and emotionally. Instead, we would spend days in silence, allowing our words, our anger, our hurts, and our frustrations to fester and build resentment within us. After a while, it felt like everything that had festered between me and Isi all this time was all that was left between us.

On the following Friday after the ball, Chance and I were having a drink after work. He was the only person I was able to open up to and, after a week of silence in my home and two Long Island iced tea drinks, I needed to talk.

"So… Isi hasn't spoken to me since the Mayor's Ball…" I casually squeezed in.

"Wait, huh? Bro, today is Friday. You mean to tell me that your wife has not spoken to you since last Saturday?"

"Yeah. It's all bad."

"So what happened? You two seemed to be getting on really well at dinner!" Chance asked with concern in his voice.

"We were! And before we got to the ball, we actually got close to really getting on," I confessed. "So how did you two go from nearly making love to total silence?"

"Kenya."

"Oh, shit," Chance said under his voice before taking another sip of his drink.

"Yeah. When me and Isi were walking off the dance floor, Kenya was there watching."

"Yoooo! That's bad," he exclaimed.. As if I didn't feel bad enough already.

"Yeah. No kidding," I quipped sarcastically.

"So, what are you gonna do now?"

"I have no clue. I'm at a loss and I feel like she's about to leave for good."

Chance and I sat together, his understanding ear at my disposal for the better part of an hour. I poured out my heart to him, telling him about how Isi and I had practically grown up side by side. I shared with him the story of our parents who, since we were toddlers, had been planning for us to marry each other. He was the first person I was able to share everything with since I was young.

Usually, it was Isi I would confide in, because she was more than just my wife – she was my best friend. But now, uncertainty clouded my heart, and I wasn't sure if I would ever be able to share everything with her again.

Ever since I set foot in America, I'd felt as though I was juggling different versions of myself for the people I cared about. For my family and Isi, I had to be the obedient Naija son, always following our traditions. For America and Kenya, I was the driven corporate lawyer who would stop at nothing to succeed. But even while playing the part of these roles, there was a small piece of myself that I kept hidden for myself. A part that was truly me.

Over the past five years, I'd been concealing parts of myself from everyone, but I found solace in Chance. He understood me in ways no one else did. As it turned out, he connected with me on more levels than I initially realized.

"When Ayana and I dealt with infidelity," Chance admitted, "she moved out and didn't speak to me for nearly two months."

Shocked, I responded, "Bro! I know you're lyin'! Chance, the brother who talked about treating women like queens and served his wife breakfast in bed every day, cheated on his wife?!"

He grinned at me because he could tell that I was actually in disbelief about it. "It's true," he said. "I haven't been the perfect husband. But we are better than ever now, because we did the work to get here."

I sat and listened to Chance talk about how he worked every day to regain her confidence. He told me how, even though she wasn't talking to him or barely looking him in the eye, he woke up every day and asked her if there was anything he could do for her. And every day she said no. He told me that, even though he wanted to go and hide and avoid her until she began to come around, he took her resistance as a sign to work harder, because she deserved a man who would fight for her.

"I began small acts of kindness and romantic gestures every day," Chance explained. "From buying her flowers for no reason at all, to keeping her gas tank filled, to writing little love notes that she would find around the house when she least expected them. Slowly but surely, she began to soften towards me again and even smiled on occasion when we were together something I hadn't seen in months."

After two months of asking his wife if there was anything he could do for her, she finally said yes and asked him to pick up eggs and milk from the store. "It wasn't about regaining her trust," Chance lectured. "I knew that would be a long way off. I wanted to first gain her confidence that I was willing and ready to do the work it would take to earn her trust again."

"I hear you, man. But 60 days of doing all that for her with nothing and no guarantee of anything in return? That must have been rough," I said in disbelief.

"My therapist put it like this," Chance responded. "If you want to be with her forever, you'll do whatever it takes to get her back, for as long as it takes. Thirty, sixty, even ninety days is nothing when you're considering forever."

"So you went to therapy too, huh?"

"Yeah. And for four months, I went by myself. I couldn't ask Ayanna to do anything with me that I wasn't first willing to do on my own. That's how important it was for me to lead in accountability."

Chance and Ayanna's journey was admirable and as much as I wanted for things to be repaired between us, I wasn't sure that romantic gestures and therapy would work for me and Isi. The depth of pain and hurt that I had caused seemed too great to overcome. Especially at that moment..

Then Chance repeated a question he asked me last week that felt different this time around. "If you're not going to give it your all, then why are you there?"

Why was I here? Why did I continue to go home to a woman that considered my every need, even while furious with me? Why did I make sure she had everything she needed to thrive here in America? Because I loved her. I'd loved her since I could form my own thoughts and ideas. I'd loved her since we became runaway kola nut bandits together. I'd loved her since she taught me how to kiss…with tongue. And for the first time in a long time, I wanted to at least try. And this time, I'd give it my all.

CHAPTER NINE

Obi

2020 was the year that tested everything. From infrastructures to economies to relationships to humanity. It was a year where many came through stronger, some came through battered and broken, and others never made it through at all–my father being one of them. My dad, High Chief Ignatius Okafor, had worked tirelessly doing whatever it took to give his family a life he only dreamed of. As his first-born child, the way I was to repay him was by becoming a man that he would be proud of. When I was younger, it was much easier to make my father proud. I did as I was told, I went to every school he dreamt for me, I married the wife he chose for me. I was the poster child for "the good son" if anyone ever was.

A large portion of my beliefs as a man were shaped by the principles my father instilled in me during my formative years. It's difficult to admit, but he was a significant factor in my struggle to embrace my true self. Yes, I'd become a grown man and I should have been able to make choices and decisions without seeking my father's approval. But in the world of Nigerian fathers, the idea of children making independent decisions often came with the significant threat the grown child being disowned or, even worse, losing the parent's respect

The thought of losing my father's respect was something I couldn't bear. So when I started discovering aspects of myself that didn't conform to my father's vision for me, I chose to keep them hidden. This often led me to question my strength and character for not strictly adhering to the path my father had set for me.

News of the severity of the Coronavirus had just broken when I received a call from my mum about my father's condition. He had fallen ill to what they initially thought was a heart attack, but it was later discovered that he had Covid-19, and the virus was causing blood clots. Within

48-hours, he'd had multiple severe strokes. I had to get to him as quickly as possible because we were told that he didn't have much time left. But the borders had all but closed to commercial airlines, and international travel was nearly impossible. Being that my father had friends in high and obnoxiously rich places, I was able to charter a private Jet to London, where my father had fallen ill. When I landed, Isi was there waiting for me with open arms and tears in her eyes.

I hadn't seen her in seven months, and I wasn't expecting for her to be able to get to London so quickly, but my heart leaped when I saw her face. She pulled me into a tight embrace and whispered, "He doesn't have much time."

"I know," I acknowledged. "But I'm glad you're here to walk with me through this." As soon as I uttered those words, I felt like trash. There I was, being comforted by my wife when I had a woman in the states who'd begged me not to leave mere hours before.

It might seem crazy to people on the outside, but Isi was the only woman I ever saw as my wife. She knew me in ways that no woman ever would— every childhood memory, every fear, every scar, and every story. I loved Isi in a way that defied possibility, but still was able to hold space for Kenya in my heart as well. Kenya had come to know me and receive pieces of me that I didn't know how to make sense of. Pieces of me that I was unable to share with anyone else. And that was the fatal flaw in the decisions I had made. Isi owned the total sum of me while Kenya only held pieces. There was an internal struggle within me that I knew I needed to rectify, and I wouldn't have any peace until I did. But not that day. That one was about my father and I needed to be there for him, for whatever amount of time he had left.

Isi

Obi's father was a man of great stature who many people feared. He was tall (six feet and four inches), had a muscular build, and looked rather menacing due to the fact that he rarely smiled at people he didn't know. However, it only took a few moments alone with him to figure out that he was one of the gentlest human beings you would ever meet. But that was the thing- few people ever got to experience alone time with the Chief.

One day I asked him, "Papa Okafaor, why don't you ever laugh?"

"Everyone does not need to know what amuses you," he replied in his thick, Nigerian accent. "As soon as people know what amuses you, they think they know what is required to take advantage of you. An actively amused person is an easily distracted person." I watched him as he paused for a few moments and surveyed the people around him. "Why don't I laugh? I simply do not show my amusement when I do not wish to be distracted."

That conversation summed up everything there was to know about Chief Okafor. He was a deliberate man who did not like to fall victim to distractions. Only one distraction managed to take him down in a way I had never seen before–Covid-19. I watched

Obi as he spent hours talking to his father, knowing it would be the last time they had together. The Chief may have appeared frail, but Obi never addressed his father in a way that would make him feel like he was less or weak. Even on his deathbed, Obi still wanted to show his father reverence. He wanted to make him proud.

I sat quietly in the corner while Obi talked to his father about his business dealings in America and shared stories of his time working for Beyoncé. I watched them laugh at how Obi made partner at one of the most prestigious and whitest law firms in Atlanta and how it perplexed the "good old boys" at work who underestimated him. But when Obi's father asked what kind of life he had prepared for his wife and his future children, the room fell silent. It was then where the Chief looked at me with tenderness and asked that I give him and his son a few moments alone.

I waited outside for what felt like an eternity until finally Obi emerged from the room in tears. I didn't know what had happened. I didn't know what had been said. But Obi stared at me with a level of intensity that made me feel warm all over. Obi stood in the doorway with tears streaming down his face for at least thirty seconds, when he grabbed my left arm and, in one swift move, pulled me into him and kissed me urgently. He held me tightly as if he was the one holding on and preparing to take his last breath. And as if on cue, a heart monitor started sounding off in the background, alerting us that his father was passing on. In those few moments, Obi's world changed forever as he faced the idea of life without his father. His compass and his guide.

We held onto each other, grappling to understand the situation during a time when everything seemed inexplicably chaotic. We didn't want to look away– to divert our gaze would feel like dishonoring the Chief in his final moments. We also didn't want to let go of each other because releasing our tight grip would mean acknowledging the harsh reality that his father was no longer with us.

We held on to each other as if our lives depended on it, our bodies serving as anchors in the tumultuous sea of emotions. The room was a flurry of activity as nurses and doctors rushed in, their desperate attempts to save him filling the room with an intense energy. Even though we both understood this was the end, I made a silent promise to myself. I would remain there, holding him, offering whatever comfort I could, until he was ready to release his grip and let go.

CHAPTER TEN

Isi

"Here's to living life fiercely and unapologetically, bitch! Cheers!" My cousin Tiwa screamed this as we toasted her on her birthday.

"I can't believe you're not celebrating your 30th birthday with a big, obnoxious Nigerian party!" I said in disbelief, but with pride in my voice as well.

My cousin Tiwa was one of the most extravagant people I had ever met. Even though she grew up in Nigeria, she embraced all things America and lived a lavish lifestyle as if she belonged here. So when she said she wanted to have a quiet dinner for her birthday, just the two of us, I was shocked.

"Pahtee, for what?" Tiwa joked, mocking our parents' heavy Nigerian accents. "I am an unwed spinstah at 30. I do not need a pahtee so people can remind me of how lonely I am."

We both laughed at the notion because, even though she was joking, the sentiment was absolutely true. Men could go their entire adult lives without being harassed about their marital status. Whereas, if a Nigerian woman was unwed by the time of 30, she was constantly reminded that her eggs were dying almost as quickly as her chance for a husband. It didn't matter how much she accomplished on her own or how well she was doing in life, a woman was nothing without a husband and a son.

"Speaking of hot sex with hot Naija men," Tiwa quipped.

"We weren't, but is this what we're doing?" I laughed.

"What? Are you getting any? Asking for a friend who is starving for healing of a sexual nature," Tiwa said jokingly. But she was also very serious about that, too.

I took a deep breath and sighed because I was ashamed to say this out loud. "We haven't done it in a while," I said shyly.

"What is a while?" Tiwa inquired. "Three weeks? Two months? One year?"

"Closer to a year," I said in shame, before taking my cosmopolitan cocktail to the head.

"Oh no! Don't avoid eye contact with me now," Tiwa demanded. "And you wonder why your marriage is hanging on by a thread!? You have a beautiful man lying in your bed and you just let him lie there?"

"I know. And a part of me, a very big part, wants him. Misses him intimately. But then I'm reminded of his betrayal and I get angry all over again. And hurt! He hurt me!"

"So what!? Right now, you just need to take your power back. Obi and that woman took something from you and I'm sure your mother has told you to withhold sex to punish him until he acts right. But that never works. You cannot make a man act right. But you can reintroduce him to the bad bitch you are and make him take notice!"

"Umm…excuse me, bartender? We're gonna need another round, please," I interrupted,because I had a feeling this conversation was going to challenge me to look at my situation differently, and I needed more alcohol to be able to digest that. "Now, tell me more about this bad bitch you speak of?"

"My dear sweet cousin. You are a beautiful, brown-skinned woman who looks like she bathes in milk and honey every day. You are brilliant and you are wise. You are not the kind of woman who sits home, cooks dinner, and cleans the house while you wait for your man to act right! You get yourself right and watch to see if he falls in line. If he doesn't, you bounce!"

"But what does get myself right even mean?! I thought I was doing everything right with Obi," I cried.

"You have to stop carrying on like a wounded puppy. Infidelity makes you feel like you have been robbed of your sense of self, your sex appeal, your…"

"My identity!" I interrupted.

"Yes. Your identity. And the only way to go and get that back is to take it by force and own it!" Tiwa lectured.

"I'm listening," I said, leaning in to signal I was really listening.

"Rediscover who you are after all this! Take up a hobby. Buy some new clothes for you, not what you think Obi would like. But for you. Take a pole dancing class, do some Kegels, and climb that tree of a husband like a spider monkey!"

I gasped and started laughing hysterically. "That all sounds glorious, Tiwa. Except for one minor issue. We don't share the same bedroom right now. I moved into the guest bedroom."

"Even better! This betrayal has made you feel unwanted and undesirable," I nod in agreement because we both know that wasn't a question. "And I'm telling you it's a lie. You are sexy and desirable, and I would bet my left nipple that your husband wants you." Tiwa was so crass. But even in her vulgarity, she was right. "You go to him all sexy and seductively, like only you can, and straddle him. Stare him in his eye for several seconds, willing him to close the distance between you. And just before he makes the next move, you do it. You close the distance yourself."

"But how will I know when to jump in and close the distance?" I asked like some inquisitive child. "You'll see it in his eyes. You'll feel it in his pants. He will go mad instantly. But in order to maintain control of the situation, you dive into him first. Because you're not there for him, you're there for you. You have a hunger and you need to be fed. Get yours. Get off. And then return to your room like a boss."

"What? Won't he feel like I've taken advantage of him?" I questioned.

"Yes. And he will love it. Trust me."

"What if he rejects me?" I asked nervously.

"He won't."

"What if he…I…" I let out a heavy sigh. "It's just been a really long time, T."

"It'll be like riding a bike. Once you get on, it will all come flooding back."

"And this is supposed to fix my marriage?"

"Oh, gawd no. Of course not! But it helps open lines of communication. You'd be surprised at how easily communication can be restored once you unclog them pipes!" Tiwa joked.

We both laughed, but I think Tiwa was onto something. I had been cooking and cleaning and trying to show Obi how much of a dutiful wife I could be, hoping it would make him appreciate me more and fight for our love. But perhaps this passive approach wasn't what we needed. Maybe it was time I took my marriage, my man, and my identity back–by force.

CHAPTER ELEVEN

Obi

After I left from having drinks with Chance, I was a bit tipsy, but I still had purpose. It was almost 9 pm, and since Isi was having dinner with her cousin, I knew she wouldn't be home until later. I walked into our penthouse condo, expecting to see Isi's bedroom light on, but she wasn't back yet. The fact that she wasn't there was perfect, because I had a surprise for her. I stopped at the store on the way home and purchased all of the roses they had left. I wanted to give Isi a night she had always dreamed of and I couldn't believe I had forgotten this. When we were in secondary school, Isi and I had made a pact to lose our virginity to each other on prom night. She dreamed of a candlelit room with a king size bed, adorned with red rose petals. Instead, we lost our virginity in the back of a town car with her corsage stuck in her hair and my boutonniere on the floor. I wanted to make that night up to her. Give her a new "first" with me. The first time for a new beginning. I wanted to make sure that Isi felt desired and loved – so I'd taken extra care with every detail.

I watched as she opened the door, and her eyes lit up in surprise. She couldn't believe it – rose petals lined the floor, leading all the way to our bedroom where candlelight flickered. Taking her hand in mine, I led her down the path of roses until we reached our destination. I opened the double doors to the master bedroom lit by soft candlelight and filled with love-soaked aromas from incense burning on either side of us. And since I wanted everything to be perfect for her tonight, I topped it all off with a '90s R&B playlist playing in the background. A necessary element.

Once we were in our bedroom, I kissed the palms of both her hands and explained what would come next. "This evening, you will enjoy a luxurious bath full of essential oils drawn just for your pleasure; I and a silk robe will be waiting for you once you emerge from the steamy water. All of that will be followed by a full body massage that is sure to melt away any tension or stress that plagues you."

Her gaze locked onto mine, intense and inviting, as though silently calling me to bridge the gap between us. There was something captivating in her eyes, a hint of a secret or a shared joke that was meant only for me. It was a look I'd come to recognize, a silent beckoning that made my heart race and my palms sweat.

Just as I was about to succumb to her silent request, to take those few steps that would bring me closer to her, she turned away. Her figure, graceful and fluid, moved towards the bathroom, the soft rustle of her clothing filling the quiet room. The door creaked open, revealing the promise of warm water and fragrant bath oils that would soon envelop her.

The image of her preparing for her bath, the way the soft lighting would play on her skin, the way the water would cascade down her body was both tantalizing and agonizing. The distance between us seemed to stretch, making the bathroom door appear miles away instead of just a few feet. I was left standing there, the warmth of her gaze still lingering as I watched her disappear into the bathroom.

I sat at the edge of the bed, my heart pounding in my chest, as I watched her undress–torturously. Slowly. She began by unfastening her jewelry and gently setting it aside, then slowly unbuttoning and slipping off the cream silk blouse that she wore. I felt the heat rising within me as she shimmied out of her black pencil skirt, letting it fall to the ground. Then I felt my breath catch as her near nakedness revealed a stunning emerald green, lace lingerie set underneath. And, oh my God…she was still wearing her high heels. I was grinding my teeth and squeezing the mattress and sheets tightly, trying to compose the ache that was growing inside of me.

My eyes traveled hungrily over her body as she reached behind herself to unhook the bra. As it fell away, I caught a glimpse of beautiful breasts coated with her creamy chocolate skin. Then she bent down, arching her back while she effortlessly slipped out of her panties, never breaking eye contact or looking away from me. I was mesmerized by every inch of her. My mind raced with fantasies about what I wanted to do to her, when Isi beckoned for me to join her in the bath.

I walked–no–rushed over to her and kissed the back of her neck. It was tempting to get in with her, but I knew she would get no rest if I did."No," I said in a raspy voice, trying to convince myself that this was the best move. "This is all for you. I want to take care of you, for a change."

After she stepped into the tub, I poured a drop of the fragrant oils into my hands, rubbed them together, and began gently rubbing her back. At first, she sat up straight with her knees to her chin, almost as if she was afraid to relax. So I bent down and put my lips next to her ear and whispered, "Lie back, my love. Relax."

I watched as she released a little bit more of herself to me by complying. "Good girl," I said. Rewarding her obedience with another kiss on her neck. This time adding a little teeth, imitating a nibble. Gentle moans escaped her mouth as I washed her, dousing her body with the concoction of oils, rose petals, and milk and honey bathwater that I had created. She sank a little deeper into the water, and I watched as her eyes rolled in the back of her head, letting me know that this was exactly what she needed, and she never had to utter a single word to confirm it.

After drying my hands on a hand towel nearby, I left Isi alone in the tub for a few moments while I went to prepare for the next phase of the evening. I opened a bottle of Merlot, grabbed the strawberries and chocolate that I had purchased from the store, and arranged them on a charcuterie board for her to have when she got out of the bath. I was just putting the finishing touches on the strawberries and chocolate arrangement when I heard her step out of the bathwater. I caught a glimpse of her glistening body as rose petals clung to her breasts and her back. She didn't bother to remove them. She simply wrapped herself up in the silk robe I had waiting for her. She was so beautiful.

When she walked back into the bedroom, I watched her eyes gleefully light up at the sight of the strawberries, chocolate, and merlot laid out for her. She glided over to the bed, propping her right knee onto the mattress, exposing the inner area of her thigh, while she carefully picked up a strawberry, dipped it in chocolate, and took slow and seductive bites. This was torture. I had almost maintained my resolve to not touch her yet, when I noticed chocolate that had dripped on her face, right next to her mouth.

"You've got a bit of chocolate on your mouth," I said while pointing to the left side of her lips. "May I get that for you?"

"Yes. Please." She whispered. And if I didn't know any better, I would have thought she was begging for something…more.

I gently took my thumb and caressed her cheek before I bent down and slowly licked the chocolate right off her face, savoring every second with my tongue. She turned to me with a look of anticipation, then she bit her bottom lip before urgently pulling me into a passionate kiss. My hands were all over her body – exploring every nook and cranny and curve as if for the first time. I felt her untying the sash that held her robe together and, before I realized what was happening, the robe fell gracefully to the floor.

As the kisses and caressing grew more intense, she began undoing my belt buckle, rushing to unleash the beast that had been growing impatient in my pants. You would think I hated myself because I grabbed both of her hands, gently but firmly, and stopped her from going any further. Because if she had gone any further, I knew I wouldn't be able to resist diving into her in an instant.

"Not yet," I whispered softly into her ear, with a hint of playfulness in my voice. "Lie down on the bed…on your stomach." She did as she was told without hesitation – clearly eager for what would happen next. "Good girl," I said, as she settled herself onto the bedspread while looking up at me expectantly through half-closed eyes.

I smiled back at her reassuringly before heading off to get everything ready for her massage. Oils fragrant with scents of jasmine and rosemary filled the room, while Avant's song "Read Your Mind," played quietly in the background.

Her warmth radiated beneath me as I began massaging her honey-soaked skin, first lightly tracing circles around her back with my fingertips before gradually increasing pressure until they were kneading deep into her flesh like dough being worked over by an expert baker's hands. With each movement intensifying as I dug into her skin, moans escaped from between those sweet lips of hers. Moans that only made me want to go harder. Deeper.

This was impossible. It was so hard to touch her like this without touching her. I had reached her thighs by this point in the massage and dammit, I couldn't help myself any longer. "I want to taste you," I said through my teeth. I didn't even realize I'd said it out loud until I saw her reaction to my words.

Almost as if she had been waiting to hear just that, she eagerly rolled over, exposing her bare breasts and creamy center to me and said, "Then taste, my love."

So I did. And with no inhibitions whatsoever, leaving behind any worries about tomorrow or yesterday, she surrendered herself to me. Fully giving herself and her body to me for the first time in what felt like forever.

CHAPTER TWELVE

Isi

"**B**iiiitch! I've been waiting for you to wake up for three hours! Where are you? How was last night? Call me or text me back NOW!" (Tiwa)

Waking up to Tiwa's antics had become a regular occurrence for me since moving to America. She kept me laughing, of course. But she also kept me in the know about how things work here. I usually responded to her text messages right away, so leaving her unread for several hours probably had her on high alert.

"Last night was pretty damn amazing. Call you later." (Me)

"Wow. So that's how it is? You are just going to leave me hanging in suspense? That's so wrong! But fine. I guess the anaconda finally got out of the cage! Hurry up and call me!" (Tiwa)

I put the phone down, grinning from ear to ear. Tiwa normally had me grinning and laughing, but today was different. I was different. My husband made love to me in a way that he never had before and I was still processing how that made me feel. I mean, sex with him felt good. And for someone that had limited experience, I would have once called it amazing. However, even though Obi was the only man I had ever been with, something about this intimate encounter with him felt different, too.

He didn't feel like the boy I lost my virginity to. His kisses weren't shy or timid. His touch wasn't unsure or hesitant. His confidence wasn't fabricated. He was a grown man that touched me and licked me and devoured me like he knew exactly what he was doing. I wasn't used to that Obi. I wasn't used to any man capturing me that way. Even after growing comfortable with each other and being married for so many years, sex usually felt measured and practical. Boring, if I'm comparing it to what happened last night. What he gave me last night was something, or perhaps someone, else.

I took deep breaths in and exhaled slowly, trying to block the negative thoughts that were beginning to surface. Thoughts that would have me wondering if she taught him these things. Did he explore his sexuality with her in ways that he never could with me? Did she give him permission to ravage her in ways that I never did? And the worst question of all, did he think of her while he made love to me? The unbearable intrusion of these thoughts would have me in tears if I allowed them to fester. So I shook those thoughts off, grabbed my silk robe that was lying in the floor, and went into the bathroom to get myself together.

Most women date and marry men that have sown their oats and gotten their sexual exploits out of the way before marriage. But for Obi and me, we were exploits for each other. At least he was mine. It had become painfully obvious that, during our time apart, he had learned new things and experienced other people. And it was getting harder and harder not to obsess over exactly how he had gotten so good at, well, everything. Regardless of how good it was to me. I took another breath in and exhaled slowly while reminding myself to enjoy the moment instead of dwelling on what might have been in the past. My husband was home with me, and I should be grateful for that. Right?

"Are those lemon blueberry pancakes I smell?" I called out

while walking into the kitchen in my red silk robe. Obi must have gotten up hours before me because I walked into the kitchen to find my favorite pancakes, chicken sausage, and potatoes all prepared for me.

"Yes, they are. I still had your mother's recipe in an old email, so I pulled it up so I could make all your favorites for breakfast," he said. Sounding ever so proud of himself.

"And what did I do to deserve all this?" I asked playfully.

"I'm glad you asked. Have a seat."

He pulled out my chair and gestured for me to sit down. I stole a kiss from his lips and then his cheek, as he carefully placed a cloth napkin into my lap.

"So proper," I teased. He chuckled as he put a plate of food in front of me, along with a glass of apple juice.

"This all looks delicious," I said. "Thank you."

"Of course. It's the least I can do," he said. It was obvious that he was trying not to look away in shame. "It's the least I could do after everything I've put you through, Isi."

"I appreciate your acknowledgment of that. More than you know."

"I also...I got you this card," he said while handing me a blue envelope. "You enjoy your breakfast, read your card, and I'll be back in a few moments. I've just got to go make a few calls."

"Ok. I'll be here," I said cheerfully.

I watched his tall, muscular frame fade into the back of the house as he walked towards his office. Then I refocused my attention back to the card he handed me. Excited, I ripped the envelope open that simply read, "my love" on the front of it. That's how he used to sign notes he would send to me when we were in secondary school.

On the front of the card, there was a painted image of a black couple embracing passionately with the words, "I still choose you."

When I opened the card it said, "Without question. Without pretense. Without hesitation. I will always choose you." My face got extremely hot from blushing and my heart began to melt at the words on the page. And even though tears were swelling in my eyes, I couldn't help taking a bite of my lemon blueberry pancake.

"How is it?" Obi asked while walking back into the kitchen.

"The pancakes or the card?"

Obi chuckled at the question. "Both?"

"Well, the card was beautiful. And the pancakes are just like my mom's. So thank you. For both." "It is my pleasure." Obi paused before continuing as if he was trying to figure out how to say what was coming next. "And I wanted you to know that I… I think I'm ready to try marriage therapy. Chance recommended the therapist that he and Ayanna went to and, if you're still up for it, we have our first appointment on Wednesday."

I didn't know how to respond to that. I wanted to cry, do cart wheels, and get on my knees to thank God, all at the same time. Instead, I jumped up to hug him and said, "Of course I'm still up for it! What changed your mind?"

"You did," he said. "You deserve a man that will fight for you. And I am man enough to admit that I wasn't fighting for you. I was fighting for a marriage but not the woman I fell in love with in my marriage. You are what's important and I'm ready, Isi. I'm ready to fight for you."

"I'm ready too. I want to fight for you. And us."

"Then let's do this," he responded.

"I can hardly wait."

Obi's eyes suddenly grew dark as he dropped to his knees and kissed me passionately. I melted as he used his full and succulent lips to tease my tongue and suck my bottom lip. Every time Obi kissed me these days, it felt like he revealed more and more of himself. And with the way he was using his tongue to lick the perimeter of my mouth and bite me, he was revealing that he was a freak of the best kind.

I was wrapped up in the warmth of his kiss when I noticed him begin untying the silk robe that covered my bare skin beneath it.

"Obi. Sweet heart," I whispered while attempting to slow my breathing and calm my senses. "What are you doing? I haven't finished my pancakes!"

"You're done now," he said with urgency and a resolved conviction that honestly turned me on. "Now open your legs and let me finish you."

I let out a sensual giggle and quipped "so much for breakfast then," as my robe fell off my shoulders and onto the chair.

My breath began to catch as he took my breast into his mouth, using his tongue to massage my areola. I let out a whimper as one, then two fingers entered me. My breathing got heavier as I tried to adjust myself to accommodate the girth of his hands. This was definitely new for me.

"Ahh!" I yelped as tension began building in my core. Obi had always been attentive to my needs and desires, but since last night, he seemed to be on a mission to please me like never before.

He kissed me slowly and passionately, taking his time to explore every inch of the exposed areas of my body with his lips and tongue. I couldn't help but moan softly as he touched me in ways that I had never experienced.

"You have got to be kidding me," I cried out as a third finger entered me.

As he continued, he became more and more aggressive. Using his thumb to gently massage my pearl, I abandoned every sense of decorum and decency as he pushed me to the brink of ecstasy. I could feel my body responding to his every touch while my mind raced with so many thoughts about how good this all felt. He ravaged my breasts, making sure to enjoy and pleasure each one equally. I panted with labored breaths, no longer able to compose myself.

My body was under some sort of pleasure spell because, "Oh my God! Obi. Fuck! Shit! I'm going to…Obi…Babe…Yes! Yes! aahhh!" My body orgasmed violently as I cried out his name and I reached my peak.

Once he was certain that I had reached the end of my pleasure sequence, he removed his fingers from my center and, one by one, licked and sucked each one as if he was finishing off a delectable meal. I was stuck in a state of shock. Panting and still trying to collect my breath and my words from the orgasm I had just experienced, all I could say was, "Wow." I had never experienced something so dangerously erotic yet so fulfilling at the same time.

Where did that come from? How had he become so expertly aware of my body without me having to tell him how to please me? I reached for his face for a kiss, hoping he would rejoin me at the breakfast table so we could talk, but he had other plans. He gently pulled me out of the chair, kissed me on the palms of both my hands, and led me to the bedroom. Where he proceeded to make love to me again. And then once more.

CHAPTER THIRTEEN

Obi

I was not a fan of therapy. I had never seen the point in lying or sitting on a couch and talking about your problems to a complete stranger. But my experience was, when one of your best friends swears by it and it seems to be the one thing that can help breathe life back into your marriage, you take a chance. Even though the horror stories of men going to couples counseling and getting ganged up on haunted me, there we were, in Dr. Julie Webster's office, on her leather, camel-colored sofa. Both of us sitting like two children who had been called to the principal's office, waiting to see who was going to begin talking first.

"So what brings you here today?" Dr. Julie asked.

Isi and I sat in silence, our glances bouncing back and forth like a silent tennis match, each waiting for the other to break the silence and speak first to the therapist. A wave of trepidation washed over me. The thought of voicing my thoughts first filled me with unease. I didn't want it to make me come across as selfish or domineering. Simultaneously, Isi appeared hesitant, too. Her eyes held a flicker of fear that suggested she was wary of seeming too eager to paint me in a negative light.

The seconds ticked by, transforming into what felt like an eternity. With each passing moment, the pressure to break the silence grew more intense. Yet, neither of us dared to take the plunge, our fears holding us captive in a standoff of unsaid words and unshared feelings.

"I understand how intimidating couples therapy can be," Dr. Julie continued. "But I promise you that this is a safe space, and nothing will surprise me or make me look at you differently."

"I cheated." I blurted out, causing Isi and the therapist both to snap their heads at me in shock. Before I realized it, I was spilling the most humiliating details of our marriage, and of my failures as a husband.

"We were born and raised in Nigeria, but Isi and I spent time apart when I graduated law school and came to America for a job. And," I paused to allow my brain to catch up with my runaway mouth, "while my wife was home waiting for me, I cheated."

"So we're just diving right in, huh?" The therapist quipped.

Her light humor helped relieve some of the tension in the room as Isi and I both seemed to drop our shoulders in relief. We each came here not knowing what exactly to expect from this process, and I appreciated the fact that Isi didn't seem like she was ready to dump all over me as soon as we sat down. She was still being the kind and dutiful wife that she was trained to be. And even though I had just exposed my harsh betrayal, Isi grabbed my hand and squeezed it as if she was trying to comfort me. I didn't deserve her.

"Isi, would you agree that this is why you're here as well?" Dr. Julie asked.

"Yes, but also," Isi paused to find her words. "I also just want us to get back to the way we were, before everything came between us."

"And what does that look like to you?" Dr. Julie inquired.

I could see Isi's wheels turning as memories began to flood

her mind. She let go of my hand, adjusted herself on the sofa, and turned to look at me with a tenderness that only Isi could.

"We used to be friends. Best friends," she said before turning to look at Dr. Julie. "I used to know everything about him. His fears, his dreams, his moods, his movements. Everything. We used to function as one organism. But now, I don't." Isi put her head down, trying to hide the tears that were forming in her eyes, "I don't know this man."

I rushed to get closer to her on the sofa and grabbed her face, attempting to look her in the eyes, but she averted her gaze.

"I'm here, Is," I said. "I'm still the man you pledged your love to."

"But you're not, are you?" The therapist chimed in. "Neither of you are the same, really. It's understandable that you both want to return to a time in your relationship where everything was great or normal between the two of you. But you both have experienced something that has changed you. For Isi, it was more of a trauma. And if you want to give your marriage a fighting chance, you both will have to commit to being different from who you were before this trauma. That starts by getting to know each other as who you are today."

Perhaps therapy wasn't such a terrible idea after all. America had indeed molded me in ways I never expected. The changes were not necessarily negative, nor did they dishonor our cherished culture. But being here illuminated the areas of my personal growth that had been stifled by living solely for my family's expectations.

I was like a boy trapped in the shadow of my father's towering presence, ceaselessly striving for success and yearning for his approval. My identity, my sense of self, was entwined with being his son – a role that often meant sidelining my own desires and aspirations.

However, if this marriage was going to survive, if Isi and I were to build a life together, I knew I had to communicate a hard truth. I could no longer revert to being that boy again, the one who lived his life through his father's lens. I needed to help Isi understand that the qualities she claimed to know and love about me were inspired by my father, not the man I have become today.

The challenge lay in conveying this transformation to Isi, in helping her see and accept the new me. The man who had grown, changed, and discovered his own path in the vast landscapes of America. The man who wanted to forge a distinct identity, not just as a son but as an individual, a husband, a partner.

We spent the next hour going over Isi's and my history together. How we met, how we fell in love, and how we fell apart. I saw Isi begin to open up more once she saw that I wasn't going to try to censor her experience in all of this. Her comfort in this room allowed the therapist to dive deeper into why we were here as all our issues came pouring out like water from a broken dam.

Every wrong move throughout our relationship felt like an elephant in the room that neither one of us wanted to address until now. I watched intently as Isi revisited her time away from me in Nigeria. How lonely she was when I wouldn't call or write. How her missing me drove her to look up my friends on social media. How that rabbit hole led her to my friends' profiles on social media. How she first discovered my relationship with Kenya. How she cried for weeks in the arms of our mothers.. How she hated me for months, threatening to divorce me. Everything else she said was expected. Warranted even. But that revelation…the fact that she was going to divorce me, broke me into pieces.

Today was the first time I was hearing how close I had gotten to losing her. And I wondered what would have become of us if she would have gone through with divorcing me. Would I have fought for her? Would it have made me return home to Nigeria to be with her? Would I have lost Kenya? It was a selfish thought but If I was being honest with myself, losing her hurt, too. No matter how twisted it seemed, it's something that hit me while

I was sitting in therapy unpacking all the issues that had eroded my marriage. I had to face the very real feelings of grief I had over losing a woman I was never supposed to love.

I didn't say much while Isi shared her experience. I Couldn't say anything at all really. As an attorney, I'd learned to be quick on my toes and always ready with a swift objection or explanation to an argument. I'd also mastered how to sit intently and listen while an opponent gave their opening statements or closing arguments in a courtroom, submitting myself to the flow and balance of due process. But this was no courtroom, and Isi wasn't my opponent. She was my partner, and the due process that I had to submit myself to in this room required me to allow my partner to unearth her pain without censorship and without my interruption, no matter how much it pained me to hear her account.

It was hard to not give any rebuttals to her account of things when it came to Kenya though. I had to bite my tongue and be silent when she called Kenya all sorts of names. Because as much as her existence hurt Isi, Kenya didn't deserve what I did to her either. I had to silence the instinct to defend myself against the accusations that I had become a liar and a manipulative person. I just sat there and ate my shame while giving Isi the safe space to unleash it all. But it was hard as hell, and I hated every minute of it.

The session ended with us being given tools by the therapist about how to rekindle our friendship first, before attempting to dive into the deep end of our love again. She recommended activities like taking walks together or going out on small trips just so there could be some sort of connection between us again, while still allowing space when needed. It almost seemed too easy. I didn't understand how taking walks or weekend getaways together was supposed to fix this enormous crater in our relationship. But she seemed to know what she was doing, and Isi was actually smiling while we dug into memories that would have most women crying their eyes out. So I guessed I'd give this a shot.

"I want you to take this journal, Isi," Dr. Julie instructed.

"When there is infidelity in a marriage and the couple decides to try to work through it, I've seen a lot of women who feel an obligation to censor their feelings. They don't want to come across as vindictive or like they are trying to throw their partner's transgressions in their face, so they never give themselves the space to honor their feelings. So when you're feeling like you've been holding on to too much or like you're trying to avoid a fight by bringing something up, just write it down. It's not to say that you and Obi won't ever talk about it. It's just so that you can honestly get your feelings out before adjusting how you deliver it to him. Does that sound good to you?"

"Of course," Isi responded quickly. "And thank you."

We walked out of the session hand in hand with gratefulness in our hearts. Dr. Julie made no promises about how things would go in therapy and, in fact, let us know that today was likely the last easy day we would have. And while I wouldn't call what I had to sit through easy, I was still prepared to take on whatever came next. I was planning on forever with her, and I had to commit to doing whatever it would take to win her trust back.

CHAPTER FOURTEEN

Isi

"Okay, so you know I have boundary issues, right?" Tiwa warned as I prepared for whatever nonsense was about to come out of her mouth.

"Yes, Tiwa. I am aware that you have no bounds or limits to your nosiness," I quipped, and we both fell out in laughter before Tiwa continued her inquiry.

Everyone has that one nosy friend or family member that has zero shame when asking probing questions, and Tiwa was mine. It was a Saturday morning and, while Obi was at the office prepping for a big merger he was lead counsel on, Tiwa and I met up for brunch and bottomless mimosas. We were on our third carafe of our orange juice and champagne delight and, for whatever reason, I had agreed to give her a play-by-play of love making with Obi. She asked questions that most people would never consider asking, while making me blush like a schoolgirl. It was embarrassing, of course. But not for the reasons that most would assume. I wasn't a prude or squeamish about sex. I just didn't have the same type or amount of experiences as most people. And this crash course that Obi was putting me through had me spinning. So I needed a trusted ear to talk to about all of this.

"When you say the sex was different," Tiwa probed, "exactly how was it different?"

"It was just very grown up. Very erotic and," I paused to try to find my words, "I guess void of inhibition?" I continued.

"So you're saying it was nasty, hot, sticky sex, then?"

"Yes. Very nasty. Extremely hot."

Tiwa dropped her head, lowered her voice, and leaned in closer as if she was preparing to tell me a juicy secret, "But did you like it?"

I hung my head in faux shame and let out a fake cry, "That's the problem, Tiwa! I think I did! I maybe even loved it! I am a nasty, sticky woman!" I exclaimed in a thick Nigerian accent.

"Ah! Ah!" Tiwa interrupted. "Let us not forget hot, my girl. You are also hot!"

I couldn't help laughing as I chronicled every hot, nasty moment that Obi and I shared. There was once a time where I would have been appalled at the idea of sharing so many intimate details of my sex life. But these were desperate times and I needed the help of my naughty cousin to decipher what this all meant.

"Madam," Tiwa chimed in with her thick Nigerian accent. "You have a man that has a

Wakanda-sized penis with the strength of the black panther, who gives you multiple orgasms, and comes home to you every night. I do not understand your dilemma!"

"My dilemma!" I exclaimed, "is that I don't know how to enjoy this pleasure without torturing myself with questions about where he learned it all from! I don't know how to be okay with this new realm of love-making when I am in constant agony, worried that he's thinking of someone else at the same time. Thinking of her!"

It was true. As much as I enjoyed sex with my husband those days, the enjoyment was always short-lived because I couldn't help but wonder if this was how she liked it, too? Did he bite her? Did he pull her hair, too? Did she do things in bed that I refused? All these questions tortured me outside the bedroom,but during sex it was an entirely different level of torture. Torture that erupted with extreme pleasure. It made me wonder, I am a crazy person aren't I?

"And what does the therapist say about this?" Tiwa dug.

I took a sip of my drink, trying to think of the best way to phrase my response.

"I... I haven't brought it up in therapy yet," I said, trying to avoid the astonishment that would soon follow.

I watched Tiwa's face turn into a frown like she was using her expression to ask me why I hadn't brought it up yet? "I know it sounds crazy, but I don't want to mess things up at home. I don't want to feel like I am complaining about the sex, because again, I genuinely love it. I just feel like, if I say enough to make him feel like I'm ungrateful, he will withdraw from me."

Where Tiwa was once laughing and making light of the situation, she now had a look of compassion on her face. She was the only person that I could be fully honest with about this, and I was grateful for her being here right now.

"You are still being so considerate of him and his feelings, as if he does not have a mountain of forgiveness to beg you for! He should be concerned about you withdrawing from him. He should be concerned about losing you. Not the other way around! Why are you so afraid of putting yourself first?"

I didn't know how to respond to that. Everything that I had been taught about being a wife failed to take me into consideration. I never really noticed that until now. Until I was at a crossroads in my life that challenged me to put aside every idea I had about marriage and being a good wife, in order to think about myself. Of course, I've indulged in the occasional self-care days. I've taken trips with girlfriends and partied my face off. But I've found myself treating those indulgences as vacations from my duties as a wife. Once I would return home, I would fall back into a rhythm of matrimonial obligation. I didn't mind. In fact, I'd always been proud of my ability to make my man feel like a king. But I'd never required Obi to take care of me with that same energy.

I explained to Tiwa how I would wake up early every morning to ensure he had his overnight oats before going to the gym. I made sure he never came home to a house that wasn't clean or a table that didn't have a meal on it for him. I'd censored my feelings about his many betrayals to ensure I didn't upset him with my hurt. And when I desperately needed to be cared for and considered, I didn't know how to ask for it. I didn't know how to demand it.

"Then you take it, my dear," Tiwa said. "It doesn't have to be some grandstand. You don't have to yell and scream for what you want or deserve. You take it by force."

"I don't know how to do that, Tiwa. I don't know how to be forceful in my stance like that. I'm not you!" I explained timidly.

Tiwa looked me in the eyes and grabbed my hand from across the table, "You don't have to be like me or anyone else. Just stop being what or who everyone expects you to be. You are more than a wife. More than an incubator for some man's seed, Isi. Maybe just start with not doing anything for Obi simply because you feel obligated and give him the opportunity to earn that treatment. And you don't do anything for him unless you desire to do it."

I sat at the table and stared out the window for what felt like hours. I wasn't not sure what I was looking for. Perhaps I thought I might find my voice out there amongst people walking around outside. People who so effortlessly did as they pleased. Then I turned back to look at Tiwa with a serious expression on my face, "the opportunity to earn me, eh?"

"Yes, my love. The honor of your love and kindness and

loyalty is an opportunity. A privilege. And once someone betrays that or takes advantage of the opportunity you so willingly gave him, he should be required to earn it."

"Wow," I responded. "I feel like you and my therapist have been having secret conversations behind my back."

Tiwa laughed and responded, "Perhaps God knew that you were too stubborn to listen to just one person's instructions. So he sent me as reinforcement."

I believed that. I sort of believed that Tiwa was sent to be an audible manifestation of my heart. When I wasn't able to find my words, when I wasn't able to give myself permission to feel, Tiwa was there.

"Remember when you wanted to be a jewelry designer?" Tiwa asked, as if I could ever forget about the dream I deferred to become Obi's wife.

"Of course I do. It was all I ever wanted to do back then."

"I just wanted to make sure because I have not seen that girl in a long time. You went to design school. You toured places like Egypt and Indonesia for inspiration. You've been featured in wearable art exhibitions! It's just hard to see you reduced to this shell of a woman who is only concerned about whether or not her crotch is smooth enough for her husband's pleasure!"

"Tiwa!" I gasped. "Why do you say such vulgar things?!"

"I am just saying. Don't you miss that woman? Don't you want to rediscover her again?"

Of course, I did. Of course, I wanted to revive the woman that fearlessly traveled the world and made art. I just didn't know how to do that while also being the woman I was always raised to be–a wife. Maybe Tiwa was right. Perhaps it was time I began to create my own reality outside of the "good girl" training my mother and aunties passed down to me over the years. Because where had it gotten me? What had it earned me except a broken heart and shattered dreams?

Tiwa and I talked for a little while longer. Each moment we spent revisiting my dreams and my passions, the more invigorated I became. In an instant, she went from being my cousin and my best friend to the best hype woman a girl could ever ask for. And when I walked out the door of the restaurant, I was committed to being someone entirely different than the woman who had gotten me to this place. After all, that is what our doctor ordered, right?

CHAPTER FIFTEEN

Obi

"What are you wearing?" I texted Isi, hoping she didn't take that question the naughty way it could come across.

"Nothing much." (Isi)

"Well, we'll get back to nothing later. For now, put on something nice and be ready in an hour. I'm taking you to dinner."

"Casual nice or formal nice?"

"Let's go with casual."

"I'll be ready."

I shut everything off at the office and locked all the doors before I stepped onto the elevator with Chance and headed to the valet for our cars.

"You and Isi have any plans tonight?" Chance asked. "Ayanna and I would love to have you two over for dinner, if you're not busy."

"I appreciate the offer, but I'm taking Isi out tonight."

Chance suddenly had a huge grin on his face while he gave me what I assumed to be a congratulatory slap on the back.

"Good for you, bro. Seems like you're throwing your full self into the work of fixing your marriage."

"I'm trying," I huffed. "It's not exactly hard in the way most would assume. Isi is amazing, and I'm incredibly blessed that she is not dogging me out the way most women would have by now. What's challenging is the fact that the therapist told us that, if we wanted to give our marriage a fighting chance, we were going to have to be different from the people we were that led us to this place in our marriage. And that was honestly a relief to me."

"Okay. So what's the problem?" Chance asked.

"The problem is that Isi is expecting me to be this traditional Nigerian man, following in my father's footsteps and becoming a chief. When in reality, I would love nothing more than to be someone completely different. I'm never going to be the guy that everyone expects. And the anxiety that comes with trying to become a carbon copy of my father is what had me hiding from her and my family all these years."

We stepped off the elevator and handed our valet tickets to the parking attendants before Chance turned to me and asked, "So why haven't you told her this?"

"Because I don't think she knows how to love this version of me."

"And yet, you haven't even given her the opportunity to fall in love with this you. What if all she is looking for is an opportunity?"

The parking attendant was pulling up with my truck when I began walking to hand them my valet slip in exchange for my keys. "Perhaps I'll start tonight," I said. Then I jumped in my black Range Rover, tipped the attendant, and drove home to take my bride to dinner.

Isi was stunning. She wore a burgundy and gold ankara pencil skirt and a gold t-shirt that was tied into a knot at the front, accentuating her full breasts. She accessorized the look with a head wrap that matched the pattern on her skirt.

"You look amazing," I said before dipping my head to pull her lips onto mine. "Those earrings. Are they new?"

"They're mine," she replied. "I mean, I made them."

"I didn't realize you were still making your jewelry."

"Well, I haven't for a while," she said nervously. "But I felt the urge today to pull some of my favorite pieces out."

"You chose well. The gold design that looks like a snake crawling around your earlobe is extremely sexy."

"Thank you. And thank you for noticing."

We got to the rooftop restaurant of the W hotel just before sunset. The sky was beautiful with hues of purple, gray, and orange, which brought out the copper tones in Isi's eyes. Everyone's eyes were on her as the hostess brought us to our table. And as we were walking, at least four women stopped her to compliment her on her jewelry. My lady was fine, black, and gifted, and I was lucky to share space with her.

"Can I get you started with anything to drink?" our hostess asked after seating us on the edge of the rooftop where we could overlook the city of Atlanta.

"We're celebrating, so can we get a bottle of Chateau Mouton Rothschild 2009 Pauillac, Premier Grand Cru?" I asked.

"Of course! And what are we celebrating?"

"I just closed the deal on a big merger at work," I bragged.

"Well, congratulations, sir. To you both. I'll have that bottle of Grand Cru brought right out."

Isi's eyes were big as she watched the hostess waltz off.

"Obi!" she exclaimed. "That's at least a thousand dollar bottle of champagne!"

"So you remember," I said in a matter of fact tone.

"Of course I remember. It's all your father ever drank on special occasions." Isi paused and smiled before continuing. "It's nice to see you incorporating the things we once loved into our lives today. I can almost feel my Obi returning to me."

I let out a gentle sigh, trying not to let what was going on in my mind show in the expression on my face. She didn't say anything wrong. It was actually pretty sweet, really. But Isi was still wanting me to be the man that my father manufactured for me, and I had no idea how to introduce her to who Obi had become.. She might not like that Obi.

"What if," I paused trying to steady the trembling that was involuntarily happening with my voice. "What if that Obi, how you remember me, is not the same as your Obi?"

"I supposed neither of us are," she acknowledged. "Dr. Julie did say that we have to be different, and I guess I'm beginning to understand that."

My heart skipped a beat when I excitedly said, "Really? You don't know how relieved I am to hear that."

"Hear what?" Isi examined. Her smile slowly faded as her eyebrows furrowed and an inquisitive look covered her face.

"I... I... I'm not the same Obi that you remember, Isi."

"That's quite obvious," she quipped.

"What's that supposed to mean?"

Isi leaned in close to me from across the table and lowered her voice. "For starters, sex with you is definitely different than I remember."

I paused and clinched my jaw, trying to keep my body from reacting as the thought of the last time I drilled into her came flooding into my brain. I chuckled softly before saying, "Yeah. I can admit that I have matured a bit in that area." It didn't even cross my mind that it could perhaps not be pleasant for her, since she seemed to enjoy the more adventurous side of my sexuality. I grabbed her chin and positioned her face so she was looking me in my eyes.

"Does that…Do I offend you when I make love to you that way, Isi?"

She smiled and bit her bottom lip shyly, which also happened to turn me on. "No. Nothing like that. I enjoy you. I am enjoying you," she said. "I was just making it known that it is different and I've noticed." She took my hand in hers and kissed the inside of my right wrist, "now continue what you were saying, my love."

I took a deep breath and continued to try to release a bit of me and my truth to her, hoping that she wouldn't reject me.

"Isi. I, I just know how much you value who you have come to expect me to be. Who everyone back home in Nigeria expects me to be. And I can't promise you that I am ever going to be that man. I don't want to be high chief in our village. I don't want to take over my father's obnoxiously large firm."

Isi looked down at her glass of champagne for a moment and, I just knew that this was where she was going to object to what I had just said and chastise me for even thinking of going against tradition and my father. My heart began to race as I prepared myself for the inevitable rejection that was sure to come.

"Is that all? Is that what you have been afraid of? What you seem to be hiding from me?" She asked softly. Caressing and tracing the palm of my hand with her fingers.

"Well, yes! Actually I thought you…" I stammered. "My father had high expectations of me. Expectations that he reinforced, even on his deathbed. And everyone, especially you, continues to inflict those same expectations on me. I guess I didn't want to disappoint you."

Isi sat and stared at me for a long time. She studied my face while she took deep, measured breaths.

"All I ever wanted was to know you, Obi. And if you changed

or outgrew something that we were once used to, I would have wanted the opportunity to fall in love with that version of you all over again. That's what love and growth is all about. We shouldn't have to pretend to be people we aren't and hold ourselves hostage to standards we no longer wish to live up to."

I sighed the biggest sigh of relief I could muster. I sighed so hard that I was nearly brought to tears. She got it. She got me. And I have no idea what had me so afraid of revealing this to her for so long. Chance was right. All Isi wanted from me was the opportunity to know me and who I was today. I wasn't doing her any favors by hiding myself from her.

"I just wish you would have trusted me with this sooner. Because if I'm honest Obi, I have been hiding pieces of myself from you, too."

"Oh, really?" I asked. "Like what?"

"I don't know. Lots of things. Some big, some inconsequential. Just things. The things that develop in a person from life experiences."

"I see," I said, not being able to stop my eyes from trying to burn a hole through that tight t-shirt she was wearing. My wife, saying that she wanted to know the man I am today, did something to my manhood. What she was saying was important, but the feeling of being received by someone I was once afraid would reject me was turning me on. Dangerously.

"What if I told you I wanted to begin making my jewelry again?" she asked, forcing me to snap out of the libido-induced trance that I was in.

"I think it would be a great idea. I remember how much you've always loved that."

"Yes but," Isi paused and squeezed my hand. I could tell that she was serious about what she was saying. "I want to do it for real this time. Start my own jewelry line and sell it. Tiwa thinks I could even put my pieces into stores. And you saw all the reactions I was getting tonight over my earrings! This could really be something, Obi."

Isi's face lit up talking about the idea of a jewelry line. Her excitement was actually infectious. But the more that idea began to sink in, the harder it became to contend with. It was a great idea and it is something that Isi had always wanted to do, in theory. But it had never been something she'd thought about seriously for a while. When Isi was heavily invested into her jewelry making, she traveled all over the world and would be gone for weeks on end. Of course she deserved to follow her dreams. I just couldn't help but, selfishly, wonder what would become of us if she started focusing on her business when we were just getting back to us and fighting for our marriage?

"What's wrong, my love?" She asked. "You seem to have gone somewhere else in your thoughts."

"I... I," I wiped my hand over my face, trying to find the right way to express the tornado of feelings that had come over me. "I just wonder if now is the best time to focus on a business when we are trying to rebuild our marriage?"

"Well, of course I wouldn't start tomorrow, Obi. I understand that this all takes planning and preparation."

"Right. A lot of planning and research and what if it gets in the way of us, Isi?"

"Do I strike you as a woman who t doesn't know how to multitask, Obi? I can assure you that I can make your overnight oats and launch a business at the same time."

Isi

Was he actually saying this? Was Obi seriously trying to discourage me from starting my own business after I had just told him that I would accept him and whoever he was becoming? After I spent years at home waiting for him while he followed his dreams and his penis wherever they led him? The audacity of this man to not see how incredibly selfish he was being!

Tiwa was right! I had spent so much time catering to him that he had forgotten that I am a person in this marriage, too! Not just some ornamental fixture in his life. I didn't get a college degree just so I could have a hobby while my husband left me home to make his dinner and clean his house. My dreams were just as important as his, and he was being a first class bastard for not acknowledging the same.

I was trying to steady my breath and fight back tears when Obi grabbed my hand, trying to recover from his obvious screw up.

"Isi, I didn't mean it like that," he said. But it was too late.

The waiter brought out our food, a steak for Obi and salmon caesar salad for me, and we ate without uttering another word to one another. What was supposed to be an evening celebrating a deal that Obi had closed had turned into a sad night in silence. We watched as people came and went, overlooking a city that seemed to be bustling with women who embraced their agency and lived the life they dreamed. Yet here I was, trapped in a nightmare of my own making because I had spent so much time devoted to becoming the image of a perfect wife. But not anymore. And never again.

CHAPTER SIXTEEN

Obi

I didn't sleep much the next two nights. Isi wasn't speaking to me and I was tossing and turning, trying to figure out what I could have done or said differently to prevent our night from ending in silence the way it did on Saturday. When we got home after dinner, Isi wouldn't even look at me. I had gotten used to her sleeping in the bed next to me recently, but after that night, she came home and moved back into the guest bedroom. I supposes I had really messed things up, but I honestly didn't think what I said was so terrible. We we retrying to rebuild our relationship, and starting a business would only distract her from that. I didn't understand why my saying as much made Isi so mad. I hung around the house, hoping for an opportunity to talk to her, but the silence had taken over our home once again.

I spent too much time in the shower the next morning, having imaginary conversations with Isi in my head. When I emerged, I was running late. Atlanta traffic was nothing to play with on Monday mornings, so I usually tried to leave the house by 6 am, before the sun was up. But after my unexpected delay, I only had two minutes to grab my briefcase and overnight oats before heading out the door. Except when I got to the fridge to grab my oats that Isi usually prepared for me, nothing was there. I rushed out into the kitchen so quickly that I missed Isi sitting at the kitchen table, calmly writing in the journal that our therapist had given her to write in. She was quiet, almost still, and didn't even bother to look up at me.

"Isi. Is everything Ok?" I said apprehensively. After this weekend, I knew everything was in fact not ok. But Isi not doing the things that she normally took pride in was taking things to a different level. And come to think of it, she didn't make dinner the previous night either. I didn't think about it because I had opted to order food. But normally Isi begins prepping dinner by noon every day, and yesterday she didn't budge! She simply wrote in her journal and stoically moved around the house. I couldn't believe I didn't notice it until that moment.. And she still had not budged to respond to me.

"Isi, did you hear me?"

"I heard you. I chose not to answer," she finally replied.

I wasn't really sure how to respond to this. On one hand, I didn't have time to try to figure out what was going on with her. On the other hand, who was this woman and what the hell did she do with my wife?!

"Isi. Look, I'm sorry for how things ended on Saturday night. But it sort of feels like something else is going on here. You're different, and I don't know what to make of it."

"Obi," she whispered. Her eyes never met mine. She didn't even bother to look up from the pages of her journal. She simply placed her pen down on the table and stared at the words on the page before continuing.

"Obi, I have spent my entire life learning how to assimilate into the role of the dutiful wife. I know how to cook all your favorite dishes. I know how you like your pants creased. I know what scents turn you on and I know what sensual moves get you off. And even after you betrayed me in the most unimaginable way, I still did everything in my power to become better for you. And I'm now starting to see that it doesn't matter. No one is checking for what pleases me or makes me happy. So I've decided to start doing it on my own. And until I feel just as much of a priority to you as I have made you in my life, make your own goddamned oats."

She didn't even give me a chance to respond. She pushed her chair back from the table, grabbed her journal and her pen, and calmly but confidently walked into her bedroom.

I arrived at work 15 minutes late thanks to my unsettling run-in with Isi. Chance was already in prepping documents for a meeting we had that day,and I was noticeably distracted. He tried to play it off like he didn't notice, but I wasn't making it easy.

"So are we gonna act like you're not over there looking like someone kicked your puppy?" Chance quipped. He knew joking was the only way to snap me out of the stupor I was sitting in.

"Am I that obvious?" I replied.

"Man, a blind man could read your energy right now! What's going on with you? Everything okay at home?"

"If by okay you mean, is the house at least still standing? Yes, everything is okay."

"And if that's not what I meant by okay?" Chance followed up.

"Then I'd say Isi has stopped talking to me and cooking for me but I'm sort of glad she isn't cooking because I can't be sure that she isn't going to poison me either."

"Damn!" Chance fired back, raising his eyebrows and looking equally concerned and amused. "What happened? I thought ya'll were solid in marital bliss?!"

I didn't know how to respond. Sure, I felt ashamed that we had managed to end back up at this place when we'd made such great strides previously. But I also genuinely didn't know what the fuck actually happened. So I took a break from the files we were preparing and explained what transpired from the time Isi and I went to dinner to this morning. Because if anyone could help me unpack what was going on, it was Chance.

"All I said was, now maybe wasn't the best time for her to be pursuing this passion project while we were trying to get our marriage on track, and she completely shut down like a child!" I passionately proclaimed.

Chance just looked at me with a blank expression, seemingly in disbelief. "Are you done?" he said stoically.

"Yes!" I exclaimed, still amped up by my indignation.

"Okay, because that was some of the dumbest and most selfish shit I have ever heard you say! Respectfully, of course."

"Bro, what? You're supposed to be on my side!"

"I don't take sides. I'm on the side of love, bruv. But still, I wouldn't touch your side with a 10-foot pole!"

"What? Why not! You think I'm wrong?"

"I think you're trippin' and abundantly wrong. That woman sat on another continent while you came to America like your name was Hakeem and sowed some royal oats! She has put her life and dreams on hold in support of you. And you mean to tell me that the first time she comes to you with goals of her own, your default response is to say to keep focusing on…you?!"

"Damn," I shot back. "I guess I didn't think about it like that."

"That's because our culture spends too much time teaching women to be perfect for men, while never teaching men how to be considerate of their women."

"Careful," I countered. "You're beginning to sound like a feminist."

Chance chuckled before explaining. "As long as I have a wife and daughters, I will be a card-carrying feminist. You'd be surprised at what your eyes are opened up to once you force yourself to consider someone outside of yourself."

After Chance finished admonishing me about all of the things I got wrong with Isi, we finally got back to work on the files we were preparing for our big case. There was a towering stack of files awaiting our attention for our high-stakes case, but my mind was a world away. I was consumed by thoughts of Isi.

I replayed our recent arguments, the harsh words, and the cold silences that had become all too familiar. The realization of how deeply I had hurt her weighed heavily on my heart. I had taken her for granted. I stopped prioritizing her needs. I stopped making her feel like her aspirations mattered. I found myself wondering, how was I going to make this right? How can I demonstrate to her that I was capable of change, that I was willing to place her needs above all else? How could I rekindle the love that had once been the cornerstone of our relationship?

The answers to these questions weren't clear, but I knew I couldn't afford to wallow in uncertainty. I needed to take action, however small, to start mending the rift between us. With a deep, resolute breath, I made a promise to myself. I would devote the rest of my days to showing Isi just how much she meant to me. No grand gestures, no empty promises, but through consistent, meaningful actions that spoke louder than words.

Tonight, I would shower her with love and affection, expressing my remorse not just in words but in deeds. I would listen to her, really listen, and remind her of the man she fell in love with. The man I was determined to become once again. It was the least I could do, the first step in a long journey of redemption. And it was a journey I was more than willing to undertake, for her. For us.

CHAPTER SEVENTEEN

Obi

The previous few times we went to therapy were a breeze. Almost too easy, if you were to ask me. We would go in with the ability to be open and transparent about our issues and we left with a sense of hope and expectation for our future. The next visit was not one of those days. It was the day I finally understood why Dr. Julie said the easiest part of our couples therapy journey would be the beginning. Because on this day, the air that filled Dr. Julie's office was thick with a tension that seemed to hum in my ears. And when she asked Isi and I how we had been since we last saw her, Isi wasted no time diving in. Her voice, usually soft and comforting, rang out harshly as she brought up our recent fight.

Her tone sent a pang through my chest. I had never experienced her like this. I mean, of course I had seen her angry. But she was normally able to remain reserved and speak with a sense of gentleness. That and her anger was usually directed towards someone else instead of me. But on thi day, Isi was unfiltered, her tongue unbridled, and her tone lacked any semblance of fucks. She was indubitably out of fucks to give.

"Isi," I started, my voice heavy with remorse, "I...I'm sorry. After that night, I had a conversation with Chance and he was able to make me see how wrong I was. He helped me see how selfish I'd been by not leaving space for you and your dreams to flourish."

There was a flicker in her eyes, a glimmer of something between hope and resentment. "Obi, I need you to reach a point where you don't need a friend to point out when you're wrong. You should be considering my feelings automatically. My needs, my wants, or my voice should never be an afterthought! "

Our therapist, a beacon of calm amidst our brewing storm, interjected. "Obi is learning to flex new muscles," she said, her gaze steady on Isi. "You both committed to change, but adjusting to this new normal will take time."

She got it. Dr. Julie understood that I had some catching up to do. While Isi was groomed to be a wife, I was groomed to be an entitled man. I couldn't simply snap my fingers and be different. I had to learn. I had to relearn her and myself for the sake of this experiment and I wasn't going to take it lightly. I also wasn't going to pretend to know it all or magically be all better for the sake of appearing to change. She needed to be willing to watch my effort and evaluate my strides accordingly. Dr. Julie said as much, and we were paying her entirely too much money for her to not know what she was talking about.

But Isi's retort came quick and biting. "Did he have to 'learn' how to love Kenya? Did he have to exercise any new muscles when it came to loving her?" The name hung in the air, a specter from my past. She knew what she was doing by bringing Kenya's name into this, I thought.

My heart pounded in my chest, the accusation stinging. "What… what does that mean, Isi?" I stammered, struggling to understand her implication. "It's not fair!"

"Are we really going to discuss the notion of fairness right now?" Isi fired back. She was really getting good at speaking her mind and not caring how her words stung.

"Before we go there and this escalates any further," Dr. Julie interrupted, "Is that a real concern you grapple with, Isi? That Obi somehow found it easier to love or be with Kenya than he had with you?"

Initially, Isi didn't reply. Her gaze hardened, her lips pressed into a thin line until finally,

"It…sometimes it is."

"Have you shared this with Obi?" Dr. Julie probed.

"No! Of course not! Look at him now. I don't even have to see his face, but I can feel his energy. He's fuming at just the mention of her name. Why would I intentionally poke this hornets nest?"

Dr. Julie looked between me and Isi for a moment before continuing. "Because it's the only way you will have your feelings validated. And it's the only way you will ever move past this." There was a few minutes of silence as Isi's breathing calmed and my heart rate reached a steady rhythm. "So try now," Dr. Julie continued. "Tell Obi about some of the thoughts that torture you when it comes to Kenya."

What was this lady doing? I thought she was on my side! But no. She set this up perfectly for me to be hit in the proverbial nuts by my wife complaining to me about my former girlfriend. Mistress. Biggest mistake of my life.

"I… I don't want to. I don't want to upset him any further," Isi began. It was the first time I heard her stern resolve soften under the weight of emotion. "I'm angry. And he's hurt me in unimaginable ways. But I still love him! And I don't want to cause him pain by speaking to him about this."

I saw a tear run down her right cheek, and all I wanted to do was rush to her side and grab her. But when I looked up and caught a glimpse of Dr. Julie's expression, she shook her head no and used her eyes to tell me to allow Isi to feel her feelings in this moment. So I sat attentively and waited for her to continue.

"Isi," Dr. Julie interjected. "Loving Obi doesn't mean shielding him from your truth or censoring your hurt so he feels better. After all, no one shielded you from the hurt that he caused you, right? Why should you be the only one left uncovered here?"

After she asked that, I realized I wasn't sure I liked therapy anymore. Was Dr. Julie trying to sabotage my marriage? Because within seconds of her coaching Isi to feel her feelings, she got a sudden jolt of courage that seemed to reignite her passionate tirade.

"Kenya. Her name, her face, her beautiful frame, her professional accomplishments…she haunts me! I see her in my dreams," Isi said. "I see her in the confident women on the streets. I see her when we make love. And…and yes, I do wonder if loving her came easier for you than loving me! I wonder if she enjoys being bitten on her nipples. I cry at the thought of her pleasuring you in ways that I never learned. I cringe when I think about you pleasuring her in the same ways you've begun to pleasure me. I am constantly tortured and taunted by this woman who has robbed me of my most intimate and most valuable possessions. And there is nothing I can do about it."

The room spun around me, the walls closing in. I could hardly breathe. It wasn't that I didn't understand that I'd hurt Isi, but it was an entirely different thing to experience that hurt. To sit there with her in it and not be able to utter a sound. I didn't know what to do with those feelings–hers or mine. As someone who had perfected the art of litigation with quick-witted rebuttals, I thought I would be able to navigate such a moment better. But there I sat–speechless. Without another word, I pushed back my chair and stormed out of the room, leaving behind the echoing silence of words left unsaid.

CHAPTER EIGHTEEN
Isi

Obi was pissed. When we were younger, he was the kind of person who you would have to do a lot for him to get upset and that hasn't changed much in him as an adult. I used to tease him and say that if someone robbed him of all his money, he would turn to them and say thank you.

"You can replace money. You can never replace a life," he'd say. And he was right.

Obi had a way with words that could defuse any argument or prevent fights from escalating. He was not one to act on his anger, a trait he inherited from how he was raised. His father had always taught him that reacting in anger was a sign of weakness. Instead, he was encouraged to embrace all his emotions, because it was too easy for men to default to anger when things got tough. This was something about him that I always admired. But don't be mistaken, Obi was no pushover. He had a fiery side to him that could be unleashed when necessary. He just picked his battles wisely, knowing exactly when to let his fierce side show.

When we were in secondary school, Alfie Nkosi tried to set Obi up on a date with his younger sister, and Obi said no. Alfie's little sister wasn't the most attractive, but Obi wasn't mean about declining. He simply said he was seeing someone else, and that it wouldn't be fair to Mary, his girlfriend at the time. Alfie didn't like that. So he started spreading the rumor around that Obi was dating his sister anyway, hoping to break Obi and his girlfriend up. And when it worked, and Mary unceremoniously slapped him at lunch in front of the entire class, Obi flipped.

Without warning or prompting, Obi stomped his way over to the giant trash bin in the cafeteria. Everyone watched as he knelt down to pick up the seemingly heavy bin, grabbing it on both sides. The bin was filled to the top with leftover food, half-drunk milk cartons, and who knows what else, but Obi didn't seem phased by that at all. Everyone watched intently as he plodded towards Alfi. And then, without a word, he dumped all of that garbage on Alfie's head. I'd seen Obi mad before, but never this mad. When he stormed out of our therapy session, the look on his face told me he was even angrier than that.

I had been saying that I was afraid of Obi withdrawing from me if I was honest about my feelings, so I wasn't surprised when that's exactly what happened. The irony of the situation wasn't lost on me, though. Him shutting me out was a stark reflection of my own behavior when I shut down to punish him, refusing to talk or communicate. I could give a silent treatment like no other, and I was proud of the amount of willpower I had when it came to holding my tongue. But watching him move around the house, not knowing what he was thinking or what he was going to do next affected me more than I cared to admit. All of this, the fighting, the mind games, the silent treatments, was getting to be too much.

Tears welled in my eyes as I fumbled for my phone, dialing the only number that could make me feel better in that moment. It was late but she was a night owl. When I was a little girl, no matter what time I woke up, she would always be up cleaning or doing something around the house. She used to tell me that she did her best work when no one was around bothering her. But tonight, I was going to have to bother her. I needed her.

I listened as the phone rang from my end. My heart was panting with nerves because I had promised her I would make the best of my time here. But I was not sure how long I could keep that promise.

Just the one word I heard when she answered instantly put me at ease, "Hello?"

"Mama," I managed to say, my voice barely more than a fragile whisper, "I want to come home." The words felt heavy, almost impossible to form as the lump in my throat threatened to choke me. It was an admission of defeat, a surrender to the overwhelming tide of emotions that had been steadily building within me.

It was as though I had been damming up these tears for what felt like an eternity. Weeks had turned into months, each passing day adding another stone to the wall I had constructed around myself. But right then, that wall was crumbling, unable to withstand the torrent of feelings any longer.

The moment those words slipped past my lips, it was as though a dam had burst. I broke down, my body trembling under the weight of suppressed sorrow and pent-up heartache. My tears, once held at bay by sheer force of will, now flowed freely, a silent testament to the pain I had been trying so desperately to hide.

Yet, there was a strange kind of relief in this breakdown. In letting go, in allowing myself to feel the full extent of my hurt, I found a sense of release. It was time to go home. It was time to heal and move on from this once and for all.

A heavy silence filled the other end of the line, my mother's response hanging in the balance. I couldn't tell if she was taken aback or disappointed by my confession. What I desperately needed from her was reassurance. I wanted her to say that it was okay to come home, that everything would be alright, and that I could pack my bags and my feelings to return. But she never did.

"Isi," she said softly, but still resolute. "Ending a marriage is far more work than fighting to keep it. At least when you're fighting to stay, you have something in common– love."

I could feel a surge of defiance rising within me. I wanted to tell her that she was wrong. That she had no idea what I was going through, how my therapist had explained that I was being repeatedly traumatized by the constant thoughts of Obi and Kenya. But before I could say another word, she dropped a bombshell that left me reeling. My father, the steadfast rock in my life, had once been unfaithful, too. He too had an indiscretion that almost shattered their marriage. But they hadn't given up. They had fought, they had remained together, they had healed. Together.

That revelation hit me like a punch in the gut, leaving me breathless and stunned. It was a side of my parents' story I had never known, a secret pain they had managed to conceal all these years. I wanted to inquire more. I wanted to dig deeper and ask her how she had managed to deal with it all. But she told me that the process of how they made it through was their journey to keep for themselves. And Obi and I would have to figure out how we would map out our healing journey for ourselves. I was still disappointed. I was even sad for them, having to overcome such a betrayal. But it also served as a beacon of hope, a tangible proof that even the deepest wounds could heal. I just wasn't sure how ours ever could.

"You need to focus on your own path now," Mama continued, her tone firm yet gentle. "Focus on mending your relationship with Obi. When you come back home, everything will fall into place, just as it should."

Her words hung in the air, a poignant echo long after the phone line had gone dead. There I was, nestled in the solitude of my quiet room, wrestling with the reverberations of my mother's wisdom and the monumental task of salvaging a marriage that seemed to be hurtling towards disaster. The enormity of it all felt like a mountain resting on my shoulders, threatening to crush me under its weight.

Yet amidst it all, my mother's belief in me, her steadfast faith, was like a beacon in this storm of despair. It was a spark, however small, that pierced through the engulfing darkness, promising me that maybe, just maybe, I could navigate my way out of this tumultuous sea of heartache and uncertainty.

CHAPTER NINETEEN

Obi

Sleep had been playing a game of hide and seek with me for the past week. It was a full seven days since that therapy session went up in smoke, and I was fairly convinced it was our last. In fact, it felt like we were in the final countdown for what remained of our marriage. Work had been relentless, keeping me away from home so much that I might as well have rented a room at the office. And Isi? I was getting the distinct impression that she was indifferent to it all.

She'd given up on cooking, and at this stage I'd stopped expecting anything different. So when I walked out of the bedroom and found her glued to her journal at the kitchen table, not even looking up to acknowledge my presence, it didn't shock or disappoint me. It was just another reminder of what our "normal" had become.

I nonchalantly strolled past her saying, "Feels like you've traded me for your journal, Isi. You're sharing more with those pages than you are with me lately." My words hung in the air, a weak effort to close the growing distance between us.

Isi didn't miss a beat, retorting, "I'm writing in this journal to find a way to communicate with you, Obi. If you knew all of the harsh thoughts swirling in my mind, you wouldn't want me anywhere near you."

This new version of Isi was like a stranger. Her once fiery spirit was replaced with an icy indifference that left me cold. I found myself lying awake at night, wondering if she still held any love for me in her heart. Was this what it felt like to watch a marriage crumble? Because after everything I had ever read or heard about the deterioration of a marriage, this was most definitely worse.

"I'm going to be working late again tonight,"I said, though I wasn't sure why. She didn't even bother to lift her eyes to meet mine, so she damn sure didn't care.

When she didn't immediately respond to my announcement, I started to walk out of the kitchen when I noticed her put down her pen and lift her eyes to meet mine. "I'll be gone this evening, too," she replied. And I was quite honestly stunned because, where the fuck did she think she was going?

"There is an art exhibit featuring Egyptian artifacts downtown and Tiwa got us tickets," she continued as if she heard my thoughts.

My gut reaction was to grill her about their plans, the protective husband in me rearing its head. But something in her demeanor suggested she was braced for my barrage of questions, almost anticipating a confrontation. I had no desire to fight with her. I wanted her to enjoy this outing with her cousin, to find some joy amidst the tension that she had become familiar with. So I said the only thing that any desperate, self-respecting husband would say, "Do you need my credit card in case you want to buy anything?"

I don't know what I was thinking. This could have easily been a setup for her to come home with a two hundred thousand dollar artifact. But my silent prayers were hoping she just wanted to buy dinner.

"Yes," she replied. "I'll take the black card."

I smirked a bit. And I intentionally held her gaze as I went into my coat pocket to pull out my wallet and grab my American Express Black card. When I placed it on the table next to her journal, I bent down to kiss her on the forehead. Then I said a silent prayer over my credit card balance and left the house for work.

CHAPTER TWENTY

Isi

The art exhibit was absolutely breathtaking. Our date began with a Town Car Tiwa arranged, waiting for me outside my condo. The sleek black vehicle was a stark contrast to the usual ride-sharing options I was accustomed to. Tiwa, ever the drama queen, had a flair for the grandiose. She was waiting for me at the museum, her eyes sparkling with excitement as she waved me over.

Our day and evening at the museum was an unexpected delight. I found myself lost in the world of Egyptian artifacts, each piece an intricate story of history and artistry. My mind was buzzing with ideas, whirling images of ancient designs reborn into modern jewelry pieces. The inspiration was intoxicating, a creative high I hadn't experienced in quite some time.

As we navigated through the labyrinth of exhibits, our laughter and chatter echoed through the hallowed halls, a testament to our girlish enthusiasm. Tiwa and I were accustomed to creating our own fun, but give us an audience and a couple of glasses of champagne and we were pure trouble. Our fun was interrupted by an unexpected encounter. A fine man, chiseled to perfection with arms that resembled rugged cliffs and a chest sculpted by Michelangelo himself sauntered over to us. He launched into the standard social script, asking about our reasons for being there and our chosen professions. All the while, his beautiful white smile and emerald green eyes sparkled with an interest that seemed to be laser-focused on me.

Tiwa was all too eager to declare her status as a social media influencer and socialite, her words ringing with an air of pride. I, on the other hand, was left grappling with a mini existential crisis as I tried to articulate my vocation. What woman, at my big age, would proudly call herself a housewife?

"My cousin here," Tiwa interjected, "is a world-renowned jewelry designer. So, you better bask in her attention now, 'cause soon you won't even be able to afford a glance her way!" We all shared a laugh, but the man's gaze remained locked onto mine, his stare intoxicating.

"A real-life artisan, huh?" he flirted unabashedly as he flashed that wickedly sexy smile.

"Yes," I managed to whisper, my voice barely audible. His attention drifted to my neck, and a blush crept up my cheeks. Was it embarrassment or something else? Suddenly, without any preamble, his thumb reached out to trace the earring dangling from my left earlobe. His other hand grazed the hollow of my neck, eliciting a shudder that rippled through me.

"These earrings, are they your designs?" he asked, his tone smooth as silk. He was the kind of sexy that was mysterious and left women longing for him hours, days after he had been gone. He didn't have to say much. His intense gaze spoke volumes.

"Ye...Yes," I stuttered, nerves getting the better of my usually composed demeanor.

"Then your cousin is right. You'll be famous in no time. You have a real gift." His words weren't just flattering; they felt like a lifeline thrown to a drowning woman. How was it that this stranger could appreciate my talent after one fleeting encounter when my own husband, my confidante for over three decades, had been oblivious to it? Sure, this Adonis could be sweet-talking me for ulterior motives, but the admiration in his eyes felt sincere, making his praise all the more potent.

I had to get some sense of control and composure back. This man was moving me in ways that I had never experienced before, outside of Obi, of course. I wasn't sure how I felt about the fact that another man could affect me this way. So when he offered to escort me to the bar and buy me a drink, I declined his offer with a polite smile, gently directing his attention to my ring finger, drawing his attention to the indication of my marital status. "Thank you, but I'm sure that's not a good idea," I said, hoping to deter his advances without causing embarrassment.

He was beyond understanding and walked away with his head high, but I had to admit, even if only to myself, that felt good. The attention and the appreciation for who I am was nice. Tiwa, ever the instigator, couldn't resist teasing me about the encounter. "He was rather cute, wasn't he?" she prodded, a mischievous grin playing on her face.

I couldn't deny it, he was attractive. "He was," I admitted, my response eliciting a triumphant giggle from Tiwa.

"But, you know," she added, her tone turning mock-serious, "nothing good ever came from a night with a light-skinned man with green eyes."

Her statement was so ludicrous, so typically 'Tiwa', that I couldn't help but break into peals of laughter. We stood there in the middle of the museum, doubled over with laughter, a pair of giddy women lost in their own world of inside jokes. Then Tiwa turned the conversation to something a bit more serious.

"If you're thwarting the advances of handsome men, then things must be okay between you and Obi," Tiwa said in the form of a statement, not a question.

"Quite the opposite," I replied. "Things actually seem to be getting worse!"

Tiwa couldn't understand how we so quickly went from barely being able to keep our hands off each other to barely speaking in the span of what felt like a week.

"Because a good marriage requires more than good sex, Tiwa."

"Ah! Ah!" She retorted. Summoning her thick Nigerian accent. "This was not just good sex, madam! You said this was mind-blowing, dirty, sticky, filthy sex! You don't just give up on something like that." We both stopped to laugh at her comedic intermission. It was just the distraction I needed to keep from crying in the middle of this luxurious event.

"I don't know if we like each other anymore," I continued. "I shared my truth with him like we discussed. I gave him the raw, unfiltered truth that plagued me and...I've never seen his entire demeanor change in an instant. And it hasn't changed back since."

"Changed like how?" Tiwa probed.

"Changed like he barely looks at me. He's quiet and calculated around me. He moves as if he doesn't trust me anymore."

"Okay, but did you talk anymore after you shared your feelings? Like, really talk to each other?" "No! I don't know what else I could possibly say."

"Anything! Everything!" she exclaimed. "I swear, you two are like the people in a frustrating rom-com where you both feel something but neither of you wants to actually communicate. It's just exhausting. You people are exhausting my entire brain!" She paused to catch her breath. And by catch her breath I mean to take a sip of champagne. "You will never know what he's thinking or how he really feels until you actually talk to the man.

And sure, he may say some things that you don't like. You will certainly say things that get his legally black boxers in a bunch. But that's what a relationship is! Saying the big, scary things that we may not want to hear but will ultimately make us better."

I hated when Tiwa made so much sense. But she was absolutely right. I was acting like the women in one of those annoying rom-com movies that we hated because everyone seemed to lack communication skills. For the remainder of the night, Tiwa and I walked arm in arm, laughing and talking about how I was going to channel "my main character" energy. It was moments like these that reminded me just how lucky I was to have Tiwa in my life.

CHAPTER TWENTY ONE

Isi

We decided to try therapy again. The familiar, sterile room of Dr. Julie's office was once again the safe haven where we attempted to mend the broken pieces of our relationship. Obi sat opposite me, his face etched with frustration and a touch of despair. His complaints about my lack of cooking and dwindling conversation came across so childish. Yet, there was truth in his words. As he spoke, I felt a surge of emotion well up inside me. Hot tears pricked at my eyes as the weight of this hurt hit like it was fresh.

I hated this. I hated feeling weak every time we tried to dig into our issues, but I couldn't help it. No matter how much time passed, every time I thought about him and her, the pain came rushing back as if I had just found out yesterday. In my heart, it didn't feel like Obi had truly paid for his betrayal and what that did to me. So admittedly, I found myself trying to force him to experience the hurt I was living through every day. And it was tearing us apart. However, in the midst of all this emotional turmoil, all this man seemed to care about were his damned overnight oats!

"Isi, have you tried discussing these feelings with Obi?" Our therapist's calm voice pierced through my spiraling thoughts.

I shook my head, barely able to choke out a "No." The memory of Obi's complete shutdown the last time I opened up was still fresh in my mind.

Obi and Tiwa were my only lifelines here. They were my nuclear family in a place that still felt so foreign. My existence had been whittled down to either hanging out with Tiwa or being planted at home, counting down the minutes until Obi walked through the door.

When things were good between us, his return was a highlight of my day. We'd exchange stories, let laughter bubble up between us, creating memories that made this foreign place feel a bit more like home. But at this point, our once warm and lively space had turned frosty and silent. So, no. I hadn't let him in on my inner turmoil. I kept my feelings tucked away, hidden beneath a veneer of calm, while inside, I was a storm of emotion.

My conversations with Tiwa plagued me where thoughts of Kenya didn't. She would nudge me to channel my inner "main character" and to stop being the constant people pleaser. I could hear her in my head, yelling for me to start prioritizing my own happiness for a change. And as long as I was in her infectious, carefree bubble, it was easy to get swept up in that idea. It felt simple to believe that I could toss aside my worries and finally put myself at the top of my to-do list. But back there, in the stark reality of our life, with the future looking like an uncertain blur, that confidence wavered. The fear crept in and the thought of stepping into the unknown, of taking control of my own narrative, was terrifying.

"I don't want to risk everything I've been trying to build here," I confessed, my voice choked with emotion. "But I don't know how to build when the embers of his indiscretions with another woman burn at the foundation of what should be our happy home."

The room fell into a poignant silence, the echoes of my

confession lingering. It was a heartbreaking admission of my innermost fears and insecurities.

Obi

My goodness, this woman had a way with words. The kind of way with words that could crush the mightiest of men in an instant. I was blindsided by Isi's confession of feeling alone. "If you'd just open up to me," I said, "instead of pouring your soul into your journal, perhaps I could ease those fears."

Isi's emotions began to surge like a tidal wave, her words revealing the turmoil within, "Obi, I don't talk to you because I don't know how to separate my love for you and my hate for what you and Kenya did!" As she allowed her feelings to spill over, her words stung as she recounted all the names she had for Kenya. A whore, a homewrecker, a godless woman…none of which truly described who Kenya was.

Dr. Julie tried to steer her towards understanding, "Isi, if you truly want to work on this marriage, you will have to learn to change your mind about how you're handling this. You will always be focused on Obi's mistake or transgression if you don't learn how to release it and give him the opportunity to rectify it. Writing in your journal is all about release. But if not done properly, you could be simply writing more of what fuels your anger and resentment. If you can't let go of Kenya and give him a chance to make amends, you'll forever be trapped in the shadow of that mistake."

But I had heard enough. I was tired of sitting there, being talked about like I was invisible and holding my tongue while these things were said. I jumped into the conversation, my words cutting through the tension, "I'm tired of hearing Kenya being labeled a whore, or you, Dr. Julie, reducing her to a mistake! Kenya wasn't a mistake or a transgression. And Isi, I'm sorry, really sorry for this, but I loved her. She didn't orchestrate this. She didn't steal from you. I willingly gave myself to her because I couldn't figure out how to be true to myself with you anymore! I couldn't show you the man I was becoming, a man who seemed to disappoint you every time I strayed from my father's path. So I found solace and acceptance elsewhere. And for that, I am sorry. But it's the truth."

My confession lingered in the air, a bitter truth hanging between us. This time, Isi stormed out of the therapy room, her sobs echoing behind her.

Fuck. What had I just done?

CHAPTER TWENTY TWO

Obi

The ride home from therapy was quiet, and you could cut the tension with a machete. But I wasn't done. Hard and more hurtful things might be said, but we needed to stop with the passive aggressive nonsense and just talk.

"Can I take you somewhere?" I asked. Not sure what her response would be after what she'd just heard come out of my mouth.

"Is it to the site of where your body will be buried in the event of your untimely death?" she quipped. And I stopped the car in the middle of the street just to look in her eyes.

"Are you being serious right now?"

"Mostly yes. But I thought we could use a little joke to break the tension, no?" I caught a glimpse of what appeared to be a smile and found myself smiling too.

As we rolled into the parking deck, I could see confusion etched on Isi's face. She had seen this building before, but never under the cloak of nightfall. I eased into my usual spot, stepped out of the car, and strolled over to her side to swing open her door.

Her eyes met mine, a question lingering in them, "Why are we at your office building?"

I smiled, leaning against the car as I told her, "I wanted you to see it at night. When it's empty, free of people with their own plans and expectations."

The building was beautiful at night, but felt different with no one there. Leading her through the quiet corridors of the building, I painted a picture for her of the stark contrast of how the building felt and looked like a typical office building during the day, versus how it seemed to look like a blank canvas at night. Full of potential and possibilities. Then I made the comparison to myself. How I too could be different when stripped of other people's agendas and expectations. Just like the empty halls of the office building. She seemed to grasp the parallel.

I showed her my office and the pictures of her and me that adorned the walls, and it seemed to soften her a bit more. Knowing that I was proudly displaying her for all to see. She felt welcomed there. As we were leaving my office, I snagged a bottle of scotch that I usually reserved for clients. Then we took the stairs to the rooftop terrace where we could overlook the bustling city underneath the full moon and glowing sky, its lights casting a warm glow across Isi's beautiful face. We passed the bottle of scotch back and forth, sipping the amber liquid as we dissected the therapy session that had just unfolded.

"Why didn't you try harder to show me who you were? Who you were evolving into?" Isi said as her voice broke the silence. I looked at her, struggling to find the right words.

"I promise, I tried, Isi. But I was scared," I confessed. "Scared of disappointing my father and consequently, disappointing you, too."

She took a long pull from the bottle before continuing her interrogation. "I would have tried. I would have made an effort to understand this new version of you."

"And now?" I asked, my voice barely a whisper, desperately seeking some sign that she might still accept me.

Her answer was a punch to the gut, "Things are different now. Before, I would have had a choice. But now, it feels like you're shoving this stranger down my throat. A stranger who has managed to hurt me in ways I can't even begin to repair. I just wish you had tried harder, Obi. Before we became…this," she emphasized. Using her hands to gesture at the imaginary crater that formed between us.

Even as she voiced her dissatisfaction, she was an exquisite vision. She practically glowed. I was at a loss for words in that moment, not knowing what I could possibly say that summed up everything I was feeling or wanted to say. So I defaulted to the only tried and true phrase that stood the test of time, "I'm sorry," I murmured, over and over again, like a broken record. "Isi, I am so, so sorry." A single tear escaped her eye, and I bent down to tenderly kiss the trail it had blazed. My tongue gently grazed her cheek, lapping up the residual tears. "I'm sorry, Isi," I repeated, my lips inching closer to hers, hovering in anticipation, praying she would bridge the gap. She did, pulling my bottom lip into her mouth, sucking with a fervor that sent shock waves through me.

A swift scan ensured our privacy on the rooftop terrace, followed by one last gulp of the scotch. The bottle cap was replaced before I set it down gently. I moved with caution, unsure of where this was leading or how it would unfold. I didn't want Isi to feel cornered, or worse, thinking this was all I craved from her. Her confession about associating lovemaking with thoughts of Kenya had thrown me off balance. So I let her take the reins, guiding me with her actions, signaling where and how far she wanted me to go.

As she stepped back, her coat slid off her shoulders and pooled at her feet. She began to unbutton her blouse, but I caught her hand, whispering, "stop." Her initial confusion was palpable; she must have thought I was rejecting her when in reality, it was quite the contrary. "Are you sure? I don't want anything from you that you're not ready, willing to give. Especially now," I said. "I just want to be here with you."

Her smile was a sight to behold, her bottom lip trapped between her teeth in a seductive bite. "You should know me by now. Offering myself to you is something I do not take lightly. I am sure, my love."

Those words were music to my ears. If she wasn't sure, the ride home was going to be painful and excruciatingly awkward, thanks to the growing appreciation for her in my pants. As she stripped off her clothes piece by piece, I stood frozen, mesmerized by her allure. My body was a barometer, displaying just how turned on I was.

Before I knew what was happening, she was sauntering towards me, a vision in purple lace lingerie and black patent leather high heels. As she traced my lips with her tongue, unbuckling my pants, I fisted a grip of her hair to pull her head back and expose her neck and hungrily taste her. Her moans of pleasure were intoxicating. Panting, I pulled back, asking, "Is this ok? Tell me you want this because…"

Before I could finish, she silenced me with a heated kiss while her right hand dipped into my briefs to grab as much of me in her hand that her tiny palm could hold. Pulling back to declare, "I want this. I want you. But I just have one question…"

"What is it? Anything," I said hurriedly.

"Has she ever been here? Have you ever made love to her here before?"

"No. Never. I promise." And I wasn't just saying that so I could get what I wanted from Isi. It was the truth. "Isi, this is something that I have only and will only share with you."

With that admission, Isi got even more excited. "Then take it," she whispered. "Don't question it. Just take it." And so I did.

With a fluid motion, I scooped her up and laid her on her discarded coat. I took, but also gave in equal measure. I tore off her lace bra with my teeth, feasting on her exposed nipple. My thumb teased her clit while my fingers explored her depths. She melted under my touch, teetering on the edge of ecstasy, pleading, "Obi! Please!"

"Please what?" I probed, daring her to voice her desires. "Tell me. I won't do anything you don't tell me to do."

She responded by gripping the throbbing hardness between my legs and stating, "This. I want this."

"Say it," I commanded. My breath heavy and needy, but confident. I wasn't going to let her off the hook. I wanted her to express herself with me, even if it made me uncomfortable.

"I want you inside me," she panted. "I want you to lick my neck, bite my nipples and devour every inch of my body while plunging mercilessly into me. Hold nothing back. And I don't want you to stop until I say so. Until I scream it. Is that clear enough for you?"

My growl was primal, the passion threatening to consume me. "Are you sure?" I challenged, eyes locked on hers as I descended to taste her sweetness. "Because I could have sworn you liked this, too," I taunted, driving her wild with my tongue lapping up her wetness and my fingers entering her center. Her squeals of pleasure echoed around us as she neared her climax.

"Obi!" She demanded, her tone authoritative. "Now." But I needed to hear her say it, to know it was okay. And then, with a sultry grin on her face. "Fuck me. Now!"

I obliged. I wasn't sure what this meant for us, but part of me was still relieved. We spent another hour on the roof. Naked. Going back and forth between moments of silence and minutes of the type of open dialogue we hadn't shared since we were kids. When we weren't talking, we were making love. It felt good to be that open and naked together–figuratively and literally. And whatever happened next, it wouldn't be due to us not talking or communicating about what was going on with us. We would be honest. We would be transparent. We would each be given space to honor our individual truths.

Isi

It was a serene Sunday morning, the kind where the sun paints golden hues on the world outside. For the first time in what felt like forever, I had the energy to whip up breakfast. Thoughts of sizzling bacon, fluffy pancakes, and creamy grits had my mouth watering and stomach growling.

But as I stepped into the living room, silence greeted me. The usual sound of SportsCenter filling the space was conspicuously absent. After we'd spent that night talking things through on the rooftop terrace of Obi's building, we'd begun to open up to each other again, rekindling a semblance of friendship. Things weren't the same, and truth be told, we didn't even know what "normal" looked like anymore. We were two strangers in a familiar dance, trying to learn the rhythm again.

It wasn't easy. We were being forced to take a good, hard look at how much we'd both changed and honestly assess if the people we're turning into were ones we could actually spend our lives with. It was hard because this decision was different from the one where we first pledged our lives to each other. As kids, we'd had a path laid out, dreams of our future together. And while I'm not foolish enough to think that plans don't change, or that people stay the same, most other couples got the chance to evolve together. Obi and I, we'd evolved and inevitably grown apart. It was hard to believe that we expected anything different. We had spent most of our married lives separate and that fact, even without an affair, was enough to tear any couple apart.

I found myself peering across the hallway, realizing that I hadn't really been on that side of the house since I moved back out of the master bedroom. Hovering there, I debated whether to knock on Obi's door or not.

"Get it together, Isi!" I muttered to myself, in what I can only describe as a rare moment of giving myself a pep talk – I'm not typically one for talking to myself. "Just put on your big girl panties, knock on that door, and see if he answers! After all, you're not a guest here, this is your home, too!" Somewhere in the back of my mind, a cheeky thought chimed in, "And who knows? Maybe he's naked on the other side!" I was spending entirely too much time with Tiwa.

I walked over to the door, tiptoeing as if I was a child trying not to wake her parents with the sound of her footsteps. I stood outside his door for a few seconds and then knocked lightly. "Obi?" I whispered, trying to respect his privacy in case he was sleeping or…I don't know. But no one answered.

I called his name again, knocking a bit harder. This time, I made sure my voice was loud and clear, "Obi! Are you there?" But still, there was no response. Tentatively, I opened the door and peeked inside, but there was no sign of him. He must have slipped out before I got up this morning.

It was quiet and all the lights were off in his room. But his bed was made, all his clothes were put away, and I could smell the remnants of his cologne still in the air. God, that man always smelled so good. I was preparing to walk out of the room when I noticed the light on his Macbook Pro illuminated. The entirety of our electronic lives was run by Apple devices because Obi liked knowing that he could retrieve documents and messages regardless of what device he was working on. Upon inspecting further, I could see that the computer screen was unlocked. I didn't have to enter a password or use a fingerprint. Everything was just there. Open. And when I peaked at the messages that were left open on the screen, I could see the last person he texted before he left the house. Kenya.

Obi

I woke up that morning with this gnawing feeling in my gut. A major reason I wasn't able to be "all in" with Isi was because of the lingering affection I felt for Kenya. Sure, things ended between us and I had zero plans of rekindling anything with her. But something in me felt like we both deserved closure. I owed her that much – answers.

Knowing Kenya to be a morning person, I sent her a text early in the day to see if she'd be willing to meet me. I would've been fine with just grabbing a coffee together in a public place. Especially considering the last time we were alone, we made love for the first and only time in the two years we'd been dating.

Before I left for London to take care of my sick dad, we'd had a pretty big fight. The cause? I'd caught her kissing her ex-husband. Even though I didn't really have any right to be as mad as I was then, I found myself on the receiving end of pleas for forgiveness and another chance. And when Kenya came over to try to mend things between us, I let things get much more intimate than we'd ever allowed before.

We would normally stop ourselves when we got to the intense kissing, other times giving in to "manual" stimulation because Kenya was so committed to her celibacy journey. She was always concerned that sex between us would cause her to get too wrapped up in a man she wasn't married to. But when she came over to beg me for another chance, she was set on going all the way and I didn't stop her. It was an error in judgment, one that I knew should never have occurred given the circumstances. Yet, there was this inexplicable feeling deep within me that suggested this could be our final shared moment of romantic intimacy. A part of me couldn't help but surrender to that emotion, despite knowing better.

When she didn't respond to my text, I made the impulsive decision to drive over to her house anyway. It was a gamble, really. She could've had another man over or not been home at all, but I was willing to risk it. I wanted to try and have this conversation face-to-face, to say goodbye to her properly.

As I navigated the streets to her house, a vivid tapestry of memories with Kenya started to unfurl in my mind. It was like one of those cinematic montages you'd expect to see when your life flashes before your eyes. Every shared laugh, every stolen kiss, every intimate conversation–all vividly resurfacing. Just the act of reminiscing about Kenya reawakened a gnawing sense of guilt, as if I was betraying Isi all over again. This is how it should have always been. I should never have allowed myself to get so comfortable with being away from my wife that the thought of another woman didn't trigger my sense of devotion and responsibility to my wife.

Suddenly, I realized how unfair this all had been to Isi. Dr. Julie had said multiple times that Isi had experienced a trauma and, even though she didn't have any interactions with Kenya herself, Isi experienced a very real type of PTSD whenever she imagined me and Kenya together. If I had a hard time not thinking about Kenya while I was driving around town, I could only imagine what being here must have felt like for Isi. It was the very opposite of fair. It was torture. She deserved a break, a spot where neither Isi nor I would always be haunted by these old memories. It was right then that everything made sense. I had to shield Isi from the fallout of my mess. I needed to get her away from the gloomy shadow of my past that seemed to pop up everywhere we turned.

When I got to Kenya's place, I found myself stuck in the driver's seat, just staring at her front door. How was I going to break the glacier of ice that had formed between us? It had been a year since we were face to face and after all the time I spent imagining this moment, now that it was finally here, I didn't know what to do or say. I tried to conjure up sophisticated words that might eclipse the harsh reality that I had dated her and loved her, all while being married to another woman. But there were no words that could soften the impact of that truth. In the end, I gave up the pointless hunt for the perfect words and decided to just go for it. There was never going to be a perfect time or some magical set of words to say what I needed to say.

With a heavy sigh, I pushed the car door open and made my way towards Kenya's front door. As odd as it seemed, each stride towards closure with Kenya felt like a step towards making things right for Isi and me.

The moment she recognized me standing on her doorstep through the window just by her door, I could tell by the wide-eyed surprise in her gaze that she hadn't expected to see me. She was there with her best friend, Jordan, and the two seemed engrossed in a deep conversation.

Clearly, I was the unanticipated ex-boyfriend who had just intruded on their intense chat, an interruption that was evidently not welcome.

"Kenya," Jordan announced, "I'm gonna go ahead and head out, k?"

Kenya's eyes widened in surprise, darting back and forth between me and Jordan. It was as if she was pleading with her gaze for Jordan to stay. But Jordan made the choice to depart, tacitly acknowledging that Kenya and I needed some privacy.

For a few tense moments, we just stood there, caught in this strange limbo where neither of us knew how to break the ice or even how to properly acknowledge each other's presence. We were suspended in a sea of uncomfortable silence, each waiting for the other to make the first move.

"Soo," I said. Using both my hands to gesture towards the inside of her town home. "Are you gonna invite me in to sit down?"

Kenya released a sigh, deep and heavy. Her expression was a complex collage of emotions, a clear testament to her internal struggle. It was obvious she was torn, and the sight of her so conflicted only amplified my guilt.

"I guess. Come on in," she finally said, her voice carrying an undertone of resignation. She moved aside, allowing the door to swing open a bit more, just enough space for me to cross the threshold.

Her posture was defensive. Not hostile or aggressive, but guarded. Even early in the morning she was stunning in one of those matching lounge sets. Beige, cable knit tank top and shorts with a matching robe. From her thick hair in a messy, curly bun to her thick thighs that threatened to tempt my resolve– she was gorgeous. But there was a palpable tension around her and it was painfully clear that I was walking on thin ice. I had to tread carefully, find the right words, and strike the right chord before she lost patience and showed me the door.

"So…what is going on that has you showing up at my house like this?" she demanded. "Did your wife finally put you out or something?"

Her question prompted an involuntary chuckle from me, because I was certain that there were numerous occasions when Isi must have contemplated doing just that. However, all I could muster was a quiet denial, "No. Isi is…"

But before I could complete my thought, Kenya interjected, her voice carrying the sting of a heartbreaking confirmation, "Your wife. Isi is your wife."

Her words hung heavily between us, a stark echo of the uncomfortable reality we found ourselves entangled in. Standing there face to face with the wreckage that I had created, I was at a loss for words. I simply bowed my head, the weight of shame pulling my gaze down. "Yeah. My wife," I confirmed in a whisper.

Kenya stared at me, her eyes welling up with tears she was desperately trying to hold back. It was clear that her need for understanding and closure was overwhelming her. Then, finally, she let go of her silence, tears streaking down her cheeks as she said, "Obi, I need to know what happened. Because for the past year, I've been replaying everything that happened between us, every conversation we had, over and over in my head. Even after finding out you were married, I still can't reconcile this with the person I know you to be. You are not this guy, Obi! You never were!"

She hit the nail on the head. If someone would have told me five years back that I'd be neck-deep in this entanglement, I would have laughed them off and called them crazy. That made Kenya's confused look all the more relatable. Yes, I was the guy who kicked off this whirlwind romance with her. But at my core, I was still the same guy who held honor and truth above all else.

The absolute last thing I wanted was to hurt Kenya any more than I already had. But I felt this burning need to lay my cards on the table, to share my raw, unfiltered truth with her—no matter how gut-wrenching it might be. I needed her to get just how much she meant to me and how our shared moments weren't just footnotes in my life. They were chapters that helped define who I was, and I wanted her to understand every word, every sentence of that narrative.

We sat there for what felt like hours as I explained to her that the traditions of my Nigerian family had made it difficult for me to pursue the career I wanted, let alone choose my own wife. I told her about how Isi and I had known each other since we were kids and how our families had promised us to each other from as early as I could remember.

I shared with her how moving to America had opened my eyes to a whole new world of experiences, but also how it had changed me into someone I feared wouldn't be accepted by my father or Isi anymore. I wanted her to understand that the decisions I made weren't because of her or anything she did. They were about me, my family, and a culture that had expectations I wasn't sure I could meet.

"So what? Now you're gonna tell me that Isi was just an arranged wife for you and that you didn't have feelings for her when you married?"

"No," I quickly rebutted. "Quite the opposite." I let out a long sigh, gathering my thoughts before I continued with my attempt at an explanation. "Kenya, the day I met you at that Beyoncé and Jay-Z concert was the first time that I considered doing something that wasn't what my father ordered. I had come to America full of Nigerian ideas and customs in my head, without ever being exposed to anything more. But the longer I stayed here, the more I began to question who I was. Question if the man I had become was really me, or if I was simply the image of the man that my father handcrafted me to be."

Kenya let out a dry chuckle, "Now that I understand."

"I know you do. And I think that's why I was drawn to you. Getting to know you and the struggles you'd had with who your father wanted you to be. I felt like you were the first person to actually see the real me. You became the reflection of the parts of me that I had to keep hidden from the expectations of my father and, ultimately, my wife.

She had a hard time understanding the idea of me hiding myself from my wife but it was true. Every time I tried to expose Isi to this new world and new ideas that I was forming, she became disappointed in the fact that I wasn't trying to become more like my father. So little by little, I hid myself from her. And the mistake I made was, rather than trying harder to get Isi to see me or understand me, I allowed my emotions to push me to hide myself in Kenya instead.

"So I was the seat-filler for the wife who you couldn't know you?" she asked,still trying to find answers to this dilemma that seemed more complex than it actually was. I tried to help her see that it was much simpler than any metaphorical explanation she could conjurc up.

"No. Kenya. You saved me. You. Your courage and strength and resilience. Watching you stand up to tradition in a way I never could...it fueled me. It gave me the strength to do the same. And I'm sorry that the only thing I gave you in return was grief. I'm sorry that the only thing I gave you was a reason to doubt how beautiful and amazing you truly are." By this point, we were both in tears.

"And now?" she asked, almost pleading with me, "What now?"

"Now, I go back to London to try to repair things with my wife. She deserves the opportunity for us to try to make it in a city that isn't stained with memories of you."

"Stained for you or her?"

"Both of us," I replied. "I just didn't want to leave without telling you how deeply sorry I am." I exhaled a heavy sigh, struggling to keep my composure as I held back the urge to break down. It wasn't because I didn't want to let her go. I knew I had to. It was the sadness in her eyes that tore me up inside. The idea that she thought she was somehow broken or that she had done something to deserve this pain. That's what was killing me.

"Kenya, I don't deserve your forgiveness, so I won't dare ask for that. But I need you to know that this–how I handled your heart had nothing to do with you. You are perfect. You are amazing. And you deserve...Kenya, you deserve everything. I will always be grateful for what you have meant to me. And a part of me will always wonder what loving you for a lifetime might have been like." With that, I kissed her on the forehead, collected my things, and walked out of the door.

Enough now. I said goodbye and closed that chapter of my life for good.

CHAPTER TWENTY FOUR

Obi

As my car pulled away from Kenya's place, an unexpected wave of freedom washed over me. Her expression when I spilled my truth and the tears we both couldn't hold back, would linger in my mind for a while. My only hope was that she would find some solace after all of this. But deep down, I knew this was necessary–a catharsis we both needed.

I wanted no ambiguity about who I was as a man in her mind. If I had to play the villain in her life story, so be it. But at least, I wanted to be the bad guy who had the guts to face his mistakes and try to set things right. Sure, dialing her number and saying all that needed to be said would have been the easier route. But that just didn't resonate with me. It felt too distant, too detached for something this personal. So I chose to confront her, to look into her eyes as I laid my intentions bare. This wasn't just about confessing; it was about baring my soul, making amends, and hopefully, selfishly, finding redemption.

My thoughts quickly shifted to Isi. I dialed her number, hoping to coax her out for a spontaneous lunch date, but she didn't pick up. A pang of disappointment hit me, but I brushed it aside. Today was about looking forward, about planning our future together. I had been genuine in every word I'd spoken to Kenya—I wanted to return to London. Just as my father designed, I wanted to take up the mantle of his practice while supporting Isi as she nurtured her budding jewelry venture. Together, we could wipe the slate clean, start anew, crafting a life molded by our aspirations and passions. This wasn't just about moving on, it was about stepping into a future that we consciously chose and designed for ourselves.

The drive home felt like a total blur – no doubt because my brain was spinning like a top with all these thoughts and plans. Before I could even catch my breath, I was already parking in front of our building. I tried calling Isi one more time, hoping she'd pick up, but it went to voicemail again. A knot of worry began to twist in my gut, throwing a shadow over my mood.

I barely had time to kill the engine before I was bolting from the car and sprinting towards our apartment. What I found there hit me like a sucker punch. Clothes tossed around like I was walking into a crime scene, drawers gaping wide with emptiness, closets echoing hollow. To anyone else, it would've looked like we'd been robbed, but I knew better. Isi was gone.

She had packed up everything, even her cherished spices she had brought all the way from Nigeria. I dialed her number three more times, each call met with the same cold, impersonal voicemail message. Feeling utterly helpless, I slumped down at her favorite spot at our kitchen table, trying to piece together what could have driven her to this extreme. Especially after the amazing night we'd just spent together.

Just as I was about to dial Tiwa's number, something caught my eye. Isi's journal lay abandoned on the table, its leather cover worn thin from countless nights of pouring her heart onto its pages. Did she leave it behind deliberately? Was it meant for me to find?

As if to answer my silent questions, I noticed a white envelope tucked beside the journal, my name scrawled across its front. A heavy sigh escaped my lips. This was some Hollywood drama level stuff. I had seen all the movies, and these kinds of letters were never good.

Obi,

I'm writing this with a heavy heart, but a clear mind. It's been a roller coaster of emotions, and I'm exhausted. Exhausted from the constant anxiety, the endless questioning -am I enough for you? How long will it take for the lure of Kenya to pull you back? And this morning, I got my answer.

I know that you woke up this morning and thought of her. And I know you went to see her. I want to say that I'm angry and disappointed, which I am. But I'm also just tired. The knowledge that she will always be the woman you can turn to, and that she is right around the corner, is enough to break me to a point of no return. And before that happens, I'm going to get off this roller coaster and end this cycle of pain and frustration once and for all.

I'm setting you free, Obi. Free to make your own choices. Choices that weren't made for you as a child.

I left my journal for you, not out of malice or revenge, but as an open book of my life. It may have seemed like I was writing into a void, instead of sharing my thoughts with you. But the truth is, I was writing *to you*. Every experience, every lesson learned during our time apart, every dream I dared to dream for our future -they're all there, a love letter of sorts. I wanted you to know me, my life, and how I too have evolved. Believe it or not, my time here with you in Atlanta has helped me to grow and see some new things about myself as well. I see what you meant by how this place can change you. And I have definitely changed.

With all that's happened, it's clear we can't rewind time. We can't erase the past, and perhaps, we're not meant to. So, I'm letting you go, Obi. Not because my love for you has dwindled, but because I love you too much to cage you in a life that might not bring you happiness. The kind of happiness she can. So I'm going back to Nigeria to begin a new chapter, a new day, full of possibilities and choices that I must make for myself.

I pray you will be well. I pray you find comfort for your heart. And I pray you find peace for your mind.

With love always,

Isi

CHAPTER TWENTY FIVE

Obi

Isi was gone. The echo of her absence reverberated through our home. I'd known, somewhere deep down, that she might leave, but the reality of it was a punch to the gut. Our last encounter had been so hopeful, so full of potential, that the sudden emptiness completely knocked the wind out of me. Even if we weren't on the best of terms.

I considered for a moment rushing to the airport, making a grand gesture like in the movies. But something held me back. A part of me knew that Isi needed space, time to process whatever she was feeling. And I... I needed time to digest the words she'd left behind in her goodbye letter. She didn't just leave me. He had left me with a choice to make and I owed it to myself to take it seriously.

In a desperate bid for answers, I turned to Dr. Julie, our couple's therapist. I hoped that maybe Isi had confided in her, given some hint as to why she was leaving. But Dr. Julie, ever the professional, only wanted to focus on me—my feelings, my reactions, and my next steps. I was resistant at first, but what was there left to lose?

We started from the beginning, from the last time Isi and

I were together. I told Dr. Julie about the car ride after our therapy session, how we'd laughed and shared a joke that seemed to lighten the heaviness that hung between us. I told her how I'd taken her to my office building and how we'd opened up to each other, baring our souls on the rooftop terrace under the starlit sky. I even told her about how we'd made love that night. I wanted her to understand how quickly and drastically things took a turn.

As I recounted the events, I could see the shock on Dr. Julie's face. She was just as stunned as I was when I told her about Isi's goodbye letter. "If you and Isi had such a breakthrough, why didn't you tell her about closing the chapter with Kenya before you went to see her?" she asked.

I struggled to find the words to answer her. I hadn't wanted to risk hurting Isi again and I wasn't sure if she would understand. But Dr. Julie was quick to correct me. "That's when you try, Obi," she said, her voice steady and firm. "You don't get to make decisions for Isi. She's not a child, she's your wife and your partner. When things get hard or when there are decisions to be made, you work through them together. Not sharing that with her beforehand showed her you didn't trust her and solidified the fact that she couldn't trust you."

Her words hit me hard, a painful truth I'd been avoiding. I wanted to argue with Dr. Julie. I wanted to tell her that my job as Isi's husband was to protect her, and that's why I didn't want to share my plans to meet with and close the chapter with Kenya. But as I found myself rationalizing my argument in my head, I realized a bitter truth – The only thing I'd been shielding Isi from was myself – my own truths and mistakes. It wasn't protection, it was evasion. Ouch!

After my soul-searching session with Dr. Julie, I found myself at Chance's doorstep. He was knee-deep in diapers and bedtime stories, doing the daddy thing while his wife was out at a political event. And while I wasn't the diaper changing type, it was a welcome distraction from …well, everything.

We cracked open a couple of beers, the familiar clink of bottles serving as an unspoken agreement to bear it all. And I found myself unraveling the tangled mess of emotions that had been gnawing at me. I even confessed to contemplating "the out" that Isi had offered in her goodbye letter. The idea of her setting off on a journey of self-discovery, while I did the same, held a certain allure. It was tempting. The opportunity to redefine ourselves outside the confines of 'us.' It wasn't an admission of failure or a signal of dwindling love. Far from it. It wasn't about seeking solace in the arms of another woman, either. Kenya was a closed chapter. This was about something far more personal.

I loved my wife more than words could express. The thought of a life without her made me sick. But paradoxically, the prospect of a life where I no longer hurt her, even unintentionally, held a certain appeal. I was exhausted, too. Not from the effort of trying to please her, but from the relentless cycle of causing her pain. We were both drained, running on fumes in a relationship that should have been our safe haven. In that moment, allowing her the freedom to rediscover herself, to find her happiness again, felt like the most loving thing I could do. It felt almost…noble.

Chance reminded me of the conversation we'd had about how he won his wife back. How for sixty relentless days, he had committed to being there for her, consistently and unconditionally. His actions weren't driven by expectations of reciprocation or rewards, but by an unwavering love and respect for her. Of course I remembered that story. It's what inspired me to fight for Isi. But when Chance posed a pointed question, his gaze steady and expectant, I faltered.

Had I lived up to my promise? Had I emulated his persistence in my efforts towards Isi? Shamefully, I had to admit that the answer was, no. I hadn't shown up for Isi with the same level of consistency and commitment that Chance had for his wife. My attempts, however genuine, had been sporadic and hesitant, at best. A stark contrast to Chance's unwavering dedication, my half-hearted efforts were a painful manifestation of my shortcomings.

"Why not?" he asked when I admitted I hadn't been consistent in trying to win Isi back.

"Every time I began a regimen of wooing Isi back, we'd have a bad day that followed. Sometimes two bad days. It was exhausting to keep going in the midst of all that frustration."

Chance just sat there in silence. He looked at me as if I had just kicked his puppy or said a mouthful of bad things about his mother. He broke the silence with a simple yet profound statement, "So, you stumbled along the way, hit a rough patch. Is that it?" His tone was far from accusatory, rather it held an undertone of encouragement. "You begin again. Each day brings a fresh chance to make things right. How does that Brian McKnight song go again? 'Start back at one,' isn't it?"

We both found ourselves laughing at his endearing yet cheesy attempt to stir up emotions with Brian McKnight's lyrics, but the truth in his words was undeniable. Setting the humorous tone aside, he then recited a familiar Bible verse, one that resonated deeply within me, "I remember my affliction and my wandering, the bitterness and the gall. I well remember them, and my soul is downcast within me. Yet this I call to mind and therefore I have hope: Because of the LORD's great love we are not consumed, for his compassions never fail. They are new every morning; great is your faithfulness." These words, lifted straight from Lamentations 3:21-23, echoed in the room.

I couldn't remember the last time I had set foot in a church, nor when I last opened my Bible. But these words provided comfort, a soothing balm to my troubled soul. They served as a gentle reminder that our missteps weren't the end of the world, that each dawn gave us a fresh start, an untouched canvas to paint a different story, to rectify the mistakes of yesterday.

After leaving Chance's house later that night, his words replayed in my mind. A sense of determination washed over me, replacing the earlier cloud of self-doubt. I knew now what lay ahead of me. It was time to hit reset, to embark on this journey once again from the very beginning. I needed to "start back at one."

CHAPTER TWENTY SIX
Obi

Over the course of the last two months, I had embraced a journey of self-discovery. The day Isi left Atlanta, my immediate instinct was to chase her down, plead for her forgiveness, and convince her to stay and give me another chance. But then I realized that perhaps this was an opportunity for introspection and growth.

Instead of pursuing her, I decided to focus inward. On me. With Dr. Julie as my guide, I wanted to use this time in my life as a catalyst for change. So, even if Isi chose not to return, I would still emerge from this experience as a better man. Better than I was before all this chaos ensued. When we first began therapy together, Dr. Julie told me and Isi that moving forward would require us to be different, and I was fully committed to that path of a different me.

With all the strategies and exercises provided by Dr. Julie, I found myself gradually learning to bravely accept who I truly was. I started by going back to the little boy who followed all the rules, and I gave him permission to imagine a future beyond his wildest dreams. I I took a week off of work and sat alone in a hotel room to map out plans for my life that weren't influenced by anything or anyone but me. For five days, I locked myself in a room and asked myself what I wanted over and over again until I curated a life that was fit for me and my desires. No one else's.

For years, I had been hiding behind a mask, a facade of perfection as the perfect son, a loving husband, and a successful lawyer. Roles I assumed because it was what my father demanded of me. But I didn't know how to be that person anymore. I barely recognized myself in him and I didn't know how to carry a legacy that didn't embrace the total sum of me. It was time I removed the mask. I had bigger goals than even my father dreamed for me and I was ready to begin realizing them.

The only obstacle standing in my way was the voice of judgment in my head, echoing my father's words of doubt and criticism. However, with all the work I'd been doing in therapy, I was learning to silence my father's judgmental voice in my head and replace it with his rare but cherished words of encouragement. Wouldn't you know it, Chance was right. This therapy thing was really working.

Even with all of this growth and self-discovery I was doing, I still grappled with a critical decision. Should I try to mend things with Isi, or should I view her decision as an opportunity for a fresh start – free from the complications and struggles that had plagued our relationship? However, before I could reach a conclusion, Isi took the decision out of my hands. She filed for divorce. The news hit me like a freight train, leaving me reeling in its wake.

While going over the turn of events with Dr. Julie in therapy, she asked if I was really surprised at Isi's decision.

"I knew it was a possibility," I confessed. "And I was being realistic about the likelihood of her giving me another chance. It was slim. I just thought I would at least get the opportunity to speak to her about the work I've been doing on my own before such a drastic step was taken."

"And what were you planning on saying to her? Did you hope she would change her mind?"

"I'm not sure. I honestly hadn't thought much beyond an apology. Because no matter what had happened between us, I didn't want our story to end with hate or bitterness, when there had been so much love between us over all these years."

"That honestly sounds like the best thing you can do for her," Dr. Julie assured. "Both of you have lived a life according to other people's demands or expectations. So showing up to see her without any expectations shows that you see her as her own person. Not just the dutiful wife that is supposed to love, honor, and obey you."

I was so grateful that I had her to walk me through this. The thought of taking a sabbatical from the firm had been brewing in my mind for a while. I toyed with the idea, contemplating if being physically present with Isi might mend our fragmented relationship. The shock of receiving the divorce papers was the final nudge I needed to kickstart my thoughts into action. I wasn't sure what the future held for us, but it certainly wasn't going to be summed up by the cold and impersonal serving and signing of a piece of paper that read, "dissolution." The only way to truly decide where we both went next was face to face. So I was going to go to her.

Chance was nothing but supportive of my decision. However, I could see a glint of excitement in his eyes – my leaving was giving him just the opportunity he'd been waiting for. He had just passed the bar exam and he was eager to step out of his paralegal role and venture into the world of practicing law. He didn't want to leave me in the lurch, so I think he was holding on to his paralegal role for my sake. What came next was a no-brainer.

The next morning I was in the office, I fired Chance as my paralegal. Not stopping there, I persuaded the other partners to welcome him into the fold as a first-year associate. The joy radiating from Chance was infectious. He was thrilled, and seeing him so happy brought a sense of contentment my way. Even if everything in my world was crumbling, seeing Chance's life be overcome by sheer joy was the best thing that could have happened in that moment.

He had always been there for me, a steadfast friend, sitting with me during some of the toughest moments of my life. It seemed only fitting that I reciprocate in some way. So, I handed him the keys to my office, telling him he could use it during my absence. I made him keep a picture of me hanging on the wall though. Just so he didn't forget who the office really belonged to.

"So you're really doing this, huh?" Chance asked. Seeming to get a bit sentimental as we were walking to the parking garage to load the last of my boxes.

"I am really doing this."

"Did you talk to the partners about your idea to expand the firm into the world of talent management?" Reminding me of the big dreams I had shared with him.

Since I had been working with so many celebrity clients, it became painfully obvious that many weren't just missing good lawyers. They needed proper management and representation. For the past year, I'd been thinking about asking the partners about creating a division for talent management, and Chance was one of the only people I had shared that with.

"Not yet," I said. "I'm trying to decide if I want to remain a partner here and launch the division or launch something entirely new on my own."

"Oh, shit! I think that's the ultimate boss move. And if you need a good lawyer on the team, you know where to find me, right?"

"Yes," I laughed. "Corner office, seventeenth floor." I joked while handing my valet slip to the attendant.

We finished talking, gave each other a brotherly embrace, and I was ready to embark on a journey with no expectations or demands. I was going to go to Nigeria and apologize to Isi. Then ask my wife to go on a date with me.

CHAPTER TWENTY SEVEN

Isi

Leaving Obi behind in Atlanta was one of the hardest things I'd done in a long time. I had gone there with plans to win him back, as if I was the one who had made a mess of things, and that was breaking me even more than anything else. I realized that I was striving to become a different person, trying to morph into someone else, as if I needed to be sorry for being myself–for being the person I'd been since day one. I hated that women often carried the burden and the stain of infidelity. I hated that we were expected to simply carry on in the name of love and forgiveness while only the transgressor got the benefits of a clean slate. The slate wasn't clean for me. The memories of the multiple times I'd had to forgive and simply forget my pain were still there, and Obi had done nothing to try to replace those memories with anything different.

That's why I had to make the unthinkable decision – a decision that broke my heart into a million pieces. I had to leave. Not just Atlanta, but the marriage as a whole. I shouldn't have to change who I was to win someone's love that had already been given to me freely. I shouldn't have been responsible for making myself more palatable simply because Obi had changed his mind about who he was. So even though it hurt, deep down, I knew that walking away was the right thing to do.

It was time for me to stand tall in my own identity, to be myself without any apologies. I couldn't let a man's incapacity to appreciate and love me for who I am tarnish my sense of self-worth. And if I was being honest with myself, Obi needed to do the same. He needed to come to a place of radical acceptance of who he was and live that out in whatever way that meant for him.

It was not lost on me that I might have had a hand in his decision to hide parts of himself from me. Obi grew up under an extraordinary amount of pressure, and I am far enough removed from the chaos now to see that there was no way he would have been able to be anything other than what his father required of him. Not without the very real fear of being disowned. There was no excuse for his betrayal. He could have made better choices. But Nigerian fathers did not tolerate being embarrassed, dishonored, or disobeyed. So Obi made the decision to honor his father over himself. An admirable choice, no matter how misguided his actions were that followed.

To many, it would have seemed utterly absurd—Obi's choice to prioritize his father's wishes over his own hopes and aspirations. But that's because the concept of unrestricted choice is deeply rooted in Western and American perspectives. American culture is built on a foundation of pleasure-seeking, freedom, and capitalism. This has morphed into a "look out for number one" mentality, which often breeds self-centeredness and an inability to shoulder responsibility for anyone other than oneself.

Contrast this with Nigerian culture, where values like honor, legacy, and loyalty are instilled in us from the cradle. Our parents toil and make sacrifices so we can stand on higher ground, enjoy better opportunities. We're steeped in a profound sense of familial pride and allegiance so deep that the mere thought of bringing shame upon our families is unthinkable.

We follow the path laid out by our parents, attending the schools they handpick, pursuing careers they envision for us. We aim for and achieve success. As they age, we repay their sacrifices by caring for them, sharing our hard-earned wealth. Then we bring up our own children, passing down these time-honored traditions and values, perpetuating the cycle. It's like a well-choreographed dance passed down through generations—rinse and repeat.

After enduring what felt like an endless journey, filled with 48 long hours of flights and tiresome layovers, I finally found myself back in the familiar surroundings of home. As the plane touched down, I felt a sense of relief wash over me – I was back in Nigeria. The familiar faces, the bustling market, the tantalizing smells of home-cooked food, and the sight of children playing soccer in the fields – it was undeniably home. At least it would be while I took the time to recharge and decide on a new path for my life.

Initially, I was planning to stay in Nigeria for good. But after giving it some thought, I decided to relocate to London. My parents' initial reaction was one of surprise, assuming that my decision was driven by a desire to follow Obi. But as I peeled back the layers of my heartache, revealing the raw truth about all that had transpired, they understood my need for change – for a fresh start.

I was going to breathe life back into my shelved dreams of becoming a jewelry designer. My journey would begin with traveling to various countries to soak up inspiration from diverse cultures and landscapes. After that, I planned to join my former roommate, Anastasia, in London. She, as serendipity would have it, was a buyer for a prestigious jeweler, and she vowed to teach me all that she knew about getting meetings with the right people who could make my career. I was ready to navigate a new path for myself. A course that was uniquely mine and not defined by Obi. It was daunting, but exciting, too.

Putting on a brave face for my family, I enjoyed a memorable dinner and drinks with loved ones I hadn't seen in ages. My mother whined that the family hadn't seen me in months, so I'd only been able to take a short nap before our home was filled with smiling, familiar faces there to welcome me home. But as the tranquility of the night settled in and I found myself in my old bedroom, the weight of everything suddenly overwhelmed me.

Collapsing onto the floor of my childhood sanctuary, tears uncontrollably streamed down my face. This was the place where Obi and I shared our deepest secrets as children, where we honed our cooking skills under our mom's guidance, and where we first whispered "I love you" to each other. Here, I mourned not just the end of my marriage, but also the loss of a bond that originated in our earliest years. In this moment, I cried out my sorrow for the husband I lost and the friendship that disintegrated as a casualty of our war.

"You are the prize, Isi." Tiwa would often say to me in our phone calls, constantly reminding me of my worth. Her words were like a mantra or a chant that gradually began to drown out my self-doubt and insecurities. Those words would have to carry me through to my next chapter. I wasn't sure how I would navigate through this storm, but I was determined to carve out a new path for myself. It was time to pick up the pieces and start something new.

CHAPTER TWENTY EIGHT

Isi

The next couple of months passed by in a whirlwind. I heard nothing from Obi. The only communication I received was a delivery of my remaining belongings and a brief note that simply read, "I'm sorry." To say I was taken aback would be an understatement. Not because I was expecting grand gestures or heartfelt pleas, but because this silence was uncharacteristic of Obi.

Obi was known for his tenacity, a man who wouldn't let go of anything without putting up a good fight. So his sudden retreat and lack of communication sort of made me worry about him. Feel sorry for him, even. Had everything that transpired between us knocked the fight out of him?

As these thoughts swirled in my mind, I had to remind myself that it wasn't my place to worry about him anymore. He was no longer my responsibility, no longer a part of my life that I had to tend to. Yet, despite that truth, a small part of me hoped that he was doing well. I wished him peace, even if that peace was found in a life without me.

Last month, Tiwa and I went to Morocco and I was so overtaken by the beauty of it all. Majestic palaces, vibrant markets, the intricate patterns adorning the architecture, and the warm hues of the setting sun painting the sky – it all seemed like a dream. A dream that I instinctively wanted to share with Obi. My best friend.

"If you're going to sulk around like a wounded puppy, why don't you just call him?" Tiwa teased. We were touring the largest gate in Morocco and North Africa, when she caught me lost in a daydream.

"I am not sulking around like a lost puppy," I said sheepishly. I searched for the right words to explain the swirling emotions I was experiencing. Even though I had promised Tiwa that this trip would be about rediscovering my inner badass, despite my efforts, thoughts of Obi continued to haunt me. Perhaps I was sulking.

Before I could respond to Tiwa's inquisition, my attention was abruptly captivated by the approaching figure of a fine, mesmerizing man. With his fair complexion, impeccable haircut, and a physique exuding strength and charm, he was a vision of perfection. His dark gray suit accentuated every contour of his muscular frame, like it was tailor-made just for him. As he walked towards us, the confidence that his posture carried made it seem like he owned the place.

"Such beautiful ladies," he charmed with his irresistible Moroccan accent. "You caught my eye as you walked the streets of the city, and I had to introduce myself. I am Aissa. And you are?"

"Famished," Tiwa jumped in. Offering her hand for Aissa to take and kiss. She was never too proud to allow a man to buy her a meal.

The man flashed us a wicked grin before dipping his head to kiss Tiwa's hand. "Well, I can do something about your current condition. But I don't feed women whose names I don't know."

I couldn't help but watch Tiwa closely as she shamelessly flirted with Aissa. There was something truly mesmerizing about her natural charm. It was as if she held a magnetic energy that drew people towards her, and it was difficult to resist her allure. The way she effortlessly captured the attention of men was both fascinating and envious.

"And you?" Aissa asked. Turning to me as if he wanted to make sure I didn't feel left out of their plans.

"Hmm? I'm sorry?" I said, as I was abruptly pulled away from my inner musings.

"What is your name and what can I feed you?" I didn't really care what he said or asked me. His thick, succulent lips framed by a neatly manicured goatee could have asked me if I wanted to go bathe in the waters of Lake Minnetonka and I wouldn't have batted an eyelash.

"My...my name is Isi," I blushed. "And I am fine with whatever Tiwa likes. I'm not picky."

"I hope you aren't just saying that so you don't appear difficult."

"I... I" I stuttered, trying to think of a clever response, but my tongue seemed to have a mind of its own. I could feel the heat rising in my cheeks as I struggled to find the words to say. Being put on the spot always unnerved me. Tiwa had this innate confidence that allowed her to speak her mind without any hesitation. I, on the other hand, was so worried about being perceived as difficult or too much that I had forgotten how to assert myself. Tiwa never had the problem, though. She always fiercely demanded what she wanted and people stumbled over themselves to give it to her.

"Just because a woman expresses her true desires," Aissa continued, "it doesn't mean she's difficult. It just means she is aware of her true power."

"See Isi," Tiwa chimed in. "This is the masculine energy that I've been trying to tell you about! He's the kind of man that won't be threatened by you going after what you want."

"Quite the contrary," Issa confirmed. "A woman who is brave enough to pursue her passions will never deter me. It would draw me closer. I find it quite sexy."

In that moment, I was both terrified and captivated by this stranger who seemed to know me better than I knew myself. He reached out for my hand, his intense gaze locked onto mine, and I felt a shiver run down my spine. It was as if he was asking for permission to delve deeper into my soul, to explore all of the hidden crevices and secrets that I had kept locked away. And I don't know what had taken over me but, I wanted to let him.

Then, without hesitation, I lifted my left hand to meet his. I was instantly lost in the warm embrace of his caramel brown eyes when goosebumps washed over my entire body as he dipped his head to kiss my hand. It was a gesture that he had done before with Tiwa, but with me, it felt different. More intimate.

His voice was like velvet. "Answer me this, beautiful Isi. What is it that you want?"

Aissa's question felt like a test to see if I recognized the strength and significance of my power. I took a step back, straightened my back and shoulders, and summoned my inner badass. Confidently, I lifted my gaze to meet his, "I want to eat. But not just a typical meal that any tourist would eat. I want to indulge in the finest and richest Moroccan cuisine, with multiple courses and endless wine. Can you deliver that, Aissa?"

"As owner of 3 of the finest restaurants in this city, I most certainly can," he said confidently. "My beautiful Isi, do you have an aversion to spice?"

"Actually? I live for it. The spicier the better." Tiwa stretched her eyes at me as if she was trying to figure out where that extra bit of confidence came from but I was equally surprised.

Then Aissa slipped his hands into his pockets and gracefully extended his elbows, inviting Tiwa and me to intertwine our arms with his. Together, we strolled down the sun-kissed path, eagerly anticipating the luxurious dinner Aissa had promised.

As we all walked together, he shared stories of his life. He was the nephew of one of the richest men in Morocco, but he didn't have the arrogance that you would expect from someone with his wealth. He appeared down to earth as he pointed out all the beautiful landmarks we passed, his vivid descriptions made it feel like we were traveling through time.

He told us how his uncle had paid for him to go to university in Ireland and even gave him a 5% stake in the country's largest bank. But despite having so much wealth, his passion was in food. I listened in awe as he told us that he had sold some of his stake in the bank to pursue his dreams, which only made me admire him more. It wasn't admiration in a romantic way, though. I admired the fearless way he spoke about making his own choices despite what people thought of him.

"Was your family or uncle was disappointed that you didn't follow in their footsteps in banking?" I asked, trying to wrap my mind around the bold way that Aissa lived and existed.

"My family would have been disappointed if I didn't pursue something that fueled me. They equipped me with the education and business acumen to make almost anything I did successful. Their greatest disappointment would have been me doing something senseless with the life that they afforded me."

So that was what it was like. Aissa was living the life that both Obi and I dreamed of and I couldn't help but wonder where we'd both be if we had that same luxury. Our families weren't royalty or anything like Aissa's, but they certainly had the means to give us permission to exist without restrictive expectations. It was refreshing to see that kind of liberation.

The rest of the evening was a blur of luxury as Aissa took us on a culinary adventure through the city in his sleek, white Mercedes-Benz. We indulged in the finest Moroccan foods and wines, each dish carefully crafted with a mix of sweet, savory, and aromatic spices. We also savored traditional dishes like couscous topped with succulent beef and lamb with a side of vibrant vegetables. And of course, no meal was complete without a refreshing mint tea to cleanse the palate. In Morocco, food is an art form, and we relished every moment of this decadent culinary experience.

As someone from a small village in Nigeria, I had never experienced such extravagance before. And for the first time in a long while, I was having a wonderful time without thoughts of Obi crashing into my mind and knocking me off balance. I must have gone four hours without thinking of him and it felt good. Aissa paid me the kind of attention that every woman deserves. He asked me about my interests, genuinely exploring what made me feel alive. He never went more than five minutes without telling me how beautiful I was. And after going through my portfolio of jewelry designs on my phone, he validated the talent that I had been sitting on for so many years.

I know this man had just met me, and it was in his best interest to flatter me and make me feel special. But something about how he considered me and paid me attention made me realize what I had been missing–courtship. I had never been courted, not really. No one has ever tried to impress me or make me feel like they were trying to prove themselves worthy of my favor. I was simply promised to someone without any consideration. With Aissa, I felt like he was giving me the choice to choose him or turn him away. But he worked very hard to get me to choose him.

After a few glasses of wine, I shared that I was going through a divorce and why. He became indignant at the thought of any man neglecting me. Vowing that with him, I wouldn't ever have to worry about such things. I was being swept off my feet in the best kind of way. But when he asked me about seeing me again for breakfast the next morning, I politely declined.

"This entire experience was amazing, Aissa," I graciously replied. "But I am still someone's wife. You deserve to spend time with someone who can be with you without the sting of guilt or regret."

"Your character is as remarkable as your beauty," he replied. Then he kissed me. First on my hand, then both of my cheeks, and sent Tiwa and I back to our hotel in his car.

That night with Aissa opened my eyes to a new way of seeing Obi. It wasn't about making excuses for him, but rather realizing how powerful it is to be truly seen by someone. It's amazing when someone looks past your flaws, fears, and disappointments, and just sees the real you. Instead of wanting to escape, they crave more of you. If you haven't experienced that kind of acceptance, you would do anything to feel it. And that night with Aissa, I almost did. But he wasn't mine, and I wasn't being true to myself. I hadn't yet figured out who I was meant to be as I embarked on a new path. And I wasn't going to let a man distract me from discovering what awaited me.

On the ride back to the hotel, Tiwa kept nudging me in my side like an annoying sibling. "So are we going to ignore the fact that you had fucking Morrocan royalty eating out of the palm of your hand?!"

I blushed, "I don't know what you're talking about, my sweet cousin."

"Bitch! Do not play innocent with me. Tell me, beautiful Isi, how did all of that attention make you feel?"

"Like royalty," I swooned. "Like a princess."

"Just as it should be, cousin. You are royalty. And if a man doesn't make you feel the way Aissa just did, then he doesn't deserve you."

I had gone to Morocco for a bit of inspiration for my jewelry, but I had come back with a bit more of myself as well.

CHAPTER TWENTY NINE

Isi

It was my mom's 70th birthday, and the entire village was coming to celebrate her. She had become the unofficial matriarch of the village because she believed in caring for anyone she saw in need of love. Sometimes love was a hug. Other times it was a warm meal. So it was fitting that all of her children, whether by blood or bound by community, came out to love on her.

As I busied myself in the kitchen, carefully simmering the goat stew for the upcoming celebration, a wave of nostalgia washed over me. The aroma of the stew, a recipe passed down through generations, stirred bittersweet memories within me. Today was also Obi's father's birthday. We used to celebrate both birthdays as a united family, the memories of laughter echoing through the house and love filling every corner warmed my soul.

We were intentional about not letting the impending divorce sever our family's bond, so Obi's family would join us today just as they did every other year. It would just be hard to see all of them without his father, the Chief. But we all vowed to not let the sting of grief ruin today. Today was my mother's day, and she deserved to be celebrated.

Obi

After four days and two canceled flights, I arrived in Nigeria. The timing of my return was unplanned, yet strangely serendipitous – it was my father's birthday. A day that used to be filled with laughter and joy, but this year, it would be the first without him.

His absence left a gaping void in our family, but as I looked at the sun setting over the horizon, casting long shadows over the home we once shared, I couldn't shake off the feeling that he had a hand in orchestrating my return, as if he had somehow guided me back here because he knew that my mother should not be alone today. Like he knew that she needed someone to hold her hand, to share stories of his life, to remember him with love and not just sadness. And whether by divine intervention or mere coincidence, I was here now.

As I stepped into our family home, I felt a strange sense of peace wash over me. That is until my mother laid her eyes on me. Then it was pure chaos.

"Obi! My son! My first-born boy!" She cried, bursting into tears at the sight of me. I hadn't seen my mum in over a year, and I wanted to surprise her. Not sure if the celebration would still be happening, I wanted to be here regardless.

"Does Isi know you're here? Are you going to the party?" She continued through sobs. Bombarding me with question after question.

"No. I am here to surprise you."

My mother's facial expression turned worrisome as she was clearly perplexed at my response. "For me? My son, what about your wife?"

"Mommy, of course I plan on seeing Isi. I just wanted to be here for you today," I assured her. "Is that alright with you?"

"Of course, my boy. But she is still your wife. And as long as your divorce is not settled, you are a husband first."

I couldn't do anything but hug my mother again and squeeze her tightly. Of course, she wasn't worried about herself. Her greatest joy was her children's happiness, and she knew that I was always happiest with Isi. I simply wasn't ready for that interaction, yet. I had gone to Nigeria with multiple items on my agenda and I wanted things to be right. Not rushed.

I grabbed my luggage and was preparing to take it into the guest bedroom when my mother grabbed my hand. "So you don't know then, eh?" She questioned, causing me to stop in my tracks.

"Know what? What are you talking about?" I probed.

She averted her gaze like she was suddenly regretting what she had started. "Nothing. I mean, the party. You know that Isi's family is still hosting a large celebration, right?"

"I gathered as much when I saw all of the aunties dressed in their most fashionable aso ebi," I laughed. Because one thing Nigerian women knew how to do was dress for an occasion.

After I put away my luggage and got myself settled in, I sat and talked to my mother for the next hour. I caught her up on my plans and what I hoped to accomplish while on my sabbatical from work.

"Your father would have been so proud of you," she beamed.

"You think so?"

"I know so," she assured me. "Your father didn't say much to you children, but his prayer was always that you paved your own path to prosperity. And look at you now, eh?"

"Really?!" I asked in shock because, I was genuinely shocked. "Mommy, everytime I tried to mention ideas different from daddy's, he always seemed to shut me down. I always thought that if I didn't follow the exact path he laid out for me, that he disown me."

"Obi," she said softly. "Your father was a proud man but his greatest joy was seeing his children come into their own as individuals. Yes, he had high standards and expectations. But this was because he was providing you with the blueprint for success that had helped him become the man he was. Obi, your father was a lawyer. And while he wasn't easily swayed by every common wind, he could always be reasoned with if you presented a good argument. All you had to do was talk to him."

It was as if she had been colluding with Dr. Julie. Over the course of my time in therapy with her, she helped me see that most of my issues in my relationships stemmed from poor communication. I knew how to communicate. But I allowed fear of rejection to keep me from communicating anything at all.

I sat with my mother's revelation for a bit and allowed it to give me a bit of peace about the future I was planning. Then I was off to get dressed in my agbada. The men's version of fancy attire for the party. Mine was a simple, two-piece blue suit adorned with gold embroidery down the middle of the shirt. If Isi slapped me in the face on sight, at least I would look good hitting the floor.

I was admittedly nervous about seeing her. We hadn't seen each other in months, and the kind of hurt and betrayal that had come between us seemed insurmountable. However, it was important for me to at least try and heal what I had broken, so I asked my mom to keep my arrival a secret while I searched for the courage to get me to the moment we came face-to-face. Once there, I wanted nothing more than to apologize for everything I had done wrong; tell her how much she meant to me; let her know that with Dr Julie's help, I was coming into myself in a way that I never thought possible; show her all the ways in which I'd grown since our last conversation.

I arrived at the party an hour after it was scheduled to start, just as people were beginning their conversations over drinks and hors d'oeuvres. It was nice being back home. Everyone welcomed me with warm hugs and smiles, as well as belated condolences for my father's passing. It was bittersweet, but also beautiful.

Moments later, Isi walked through the door. As soon as our eyes met, time seemed to stand still around us. I stared, taking every bit of her into account from head-to-toe which made me realize just how much she meant to me, not to mention how stunning she was. But then something caught my eye. I couldn't be sure and I was absolutely jet lagged, so perhaps I was imagining things. But was that a bump? A belly?

CHAPTER THIRTY

Isi

Things took an unexpected turn during my travels so I ended up coming home early. Our last week in Morocco, just before we were scheduled to head to Abu Dhabi, I found myself sick, unable to leave my room, let alone the bathroom the entire week. I initially didn't think much of it, but Tiwa kept making jokes about me giving birth to a big headed, baby Mandigo and it stopped me dead in my tracks. During all the traveling and sheer excitement of my new-found freedom, I hadn't had a period. Could I be? Was I pregnant?

"You spent months in the house getting dicked down by the good Juris Doctor and you didn't for one minute think you could get pregnant?" Tiwa lectured while smacking her lips.

Of course, I knew it was possible. We had made love, vigorously, several times, and not once with protection. I guess I was so caught up in our attempt to repair things that I didn't think about the consequences of potentially bringing a baby into our drama. I was honestly just happy to feel wanted and desired by my husband after so long.

Being a woman in a foreign country was a scary experience.

Without being sure of customs and how things worked when it came to issues of the feminine nature, I wasn't sure how I was going to find out if I actually was pregnant. So instead of going on an embarrassing quest to locate a home pregnancy test, I simply went to a local doctor and took a blood test. Within thirty minutes, my suspicions were confirmed. I was pregnant. Fifteen weeks pregnant, to be exact. And I immediately knew when it happened. The night Tiwa encouraged me to go home and reclaim my man and take my marriage back by force. As it turned out, I took more than I bargained for. So instead of continuing my travels, I went home.

Despite this detour, I was still planning to move to London. I was keeping the baby, and I had every intention of telling Obi, but I needed time to wrap my mind around it all. My mother disagreed with my not telling Obi right away. She felt like this was God's way of giving me and Obi something to fight for. But I disagreed.

Even though I believed babies were a blessing, it didn't mean that they were miracle workers. Too many times I'd seen couples bring new life into the world as a last-ditch effort to save a dying marriage, and it was almost always devastating. I didn't want that for me or my child. My child would be loved. She would be cherished. But she would not be a tool. So I waited and decided that I would tell Obi when I was ready. Only I wasn't expecting to see him tonight. Suddenly, my well-thought-out plan was crumbling before my eyes. Obi was here. He would likely have questions. But my God did he look good.

CHAPTER THIRTY ONE

Obi

When I finally pulled myself together enough to speak after what felt like hours (but were mere seconds), all I could say was, "Hey."

Isi just smiled warmly, "Hi, Obi. It's good to see you. We… we should talk." Then she grabbed me by the hand and led me to the terrace outside her parents' house, away from the crowd and inquisitive stares. I was still mostly speechless, so I just went along with her.

We both sat quietly on a bench, neither of us sure what to say in that moment. "How long have you been here?" she asked.

How long have you been pregnant? Is what I wanted to ask but that was a bit too intense for now. "I just arrived today. I wanted to surprise my mum." I let a few moments pass to watch the expression on her face. I wanted to see if she actually wanted me to want to see her. And as I saw the expectant expression on her face begin to fade, I said, "And you. I was hoping to see you, too."

She smiled. "I'm not sure who was more surprised, though. Me or you?" she said jokingly.

I smirked, not wanting to respond right away because honestly,

I wasn't sure who was more surprised either. The tension and apprehension of the moment had us both in a choke hold, so we just sat quietly, sipping our drinks until I eventually found courage to whisper out, "Why didn't you tell me?"

I had unexpected tears watering my eyes and emotion trapped in my throat when she reached over to grab my hand to place it on her growing belly. "Because if we were ever going to give us another try, I wanted it to be because you wanted me. Not out of some parental obligation. We both have had enough of that to last us a lifetime."

As angry and upset as I wanted to be, I couldn't be because she was right. I would have dropped everything to be by her side, and it wouldn't have taken any time for me to assimilate back into the dutiful role that I had been groomed for.

"Are you up for taking a walk with me?" I asked. I wanted to take some time retracing the steps of our childhood. This didn't feel like a coincidence, and I felt the urge to savor every moment, where it all began.

Isi looked at me with a big grin, "Sure. I'd love to." Then I stood and held my hand out to help her up and off the bench.

We started off slowly, walking past the house I grew up in and laughing at all the memories that seemed to come flooding back. I had avoided talks of the past with Isi before, thinking that the memories would be more painful than helpful. But I was wrong. I needed the reminder of not just my time with Isi, but also my father. There was so much more to him than the stiff tradition and wisdom of the ages. He was my friend. And when I didn't have anything left of him, the memories kept him with me.

"Do you remember the day my father passed away? When he sent you out of the room so we could talk?" Isi didn't say anything back, but the tears in her eyes confirmed she was immediately transported back to that day.

"He knew he didn't have much time left. He also knew about

Kenya. I had never been so ashamed in all my life. Frail and weak, he looked me in the eye and told me that I needed to make a decision about the kind of man I wanted my children to see when they looked at me. 'Children don't care what you say. They will watch your character and judge you accordingly,' he said. He reminded me that you weren't simply chosen for me as a wife, but that I was granted stewardship over you. And that I would be responsible for how I presented you back to God. His last words to me were, 'What condition will God receive your wife in?'"

"Wow," was the only word that Isi could muster, but our bond was such that we rarely needed words. Even in his death, my father was still looking out for his legacy. The legacy that Isi was now carrying.

"Isi," I continued. "Will you forgive me? I don't need you to take me back. I don't expect you to. But I can't have our relationship be plagued by resentment and bitterness. I miss my best friend."

"I have already forgiven you, Obi. I forgave you the day I left Atlanta, and I've missed you every day since."

"Say it again," I demanded. "Tell me you've missed me every day again, please?"

And without warning, she lunged at me, got on her tiptoes to wrap both arms around my neck, and planted the biggest kiss on my lips. It started out funny and playful with how she jumped into my arms. Then her smile faded a bit as she gently placed her hands on both sides of my face and just stared me in the eyes. "Tell me what you want, Obi."

I didn't hesitate. I didn't ask her to clarify or state what she meant by the question. And I didn't consider what anyone else might think of what I would say. "I want you. To get to know you. To court you. I want to marry you. I want the family that I have begun with you. I want to create a legacy with you. I want to chart new courses with you. Only you"

"What if I still wanted a divorce?" she asked.

I wasn't sure how to take that question because she was smiling when she asked. And then her reason for still wanting a divorce struck me like a bolt of lightning. "That's fine," I said. "Under one condition."

"What?" she asked expectantly.

"I'd like to take you out some time. Would you go on a date with me?"

Isi and I had been joined together by a marriage of tradition. This next time around, it would have to be a marriage that we had both chosen. Where we were free to make our own rules and create our own traditions.

She pulled my face to hers and kissed my forehead, then softly kissed my lips. "Yes. I'd love to go on a date with you."

The rest of the evening passed by quickly as we walked through town, talking about memories both old and new. By the time we had made it back to her house, it was just the two of us. And although nothing else occurred that night beyond the talking, I remember feeling happy and content, but also excited, wondering if perhaps this might be the start of something new. I was excited to find out. So I woke up the next morning, got myself dressed and took my wife out on a date. It was the first day of our newly defined forever. Day one.

THE END